CW00828924

Copyright © 2017 by Matt Shaw

Matt Shaw Publications

All rights reserved. This book or any portion thereof

may not be reproduced or used in any manner whatsoever

without the express written permission of the publisher

except for the use of brief quotations in a book review.

The characters in this book are purely fictitious.

Any likeness to persons living or dead is purely coincidental.

www.mattshawpublications.co.uk

www.facebook.com/mattshawpublications

The Game

Matt Shaw

PART ONE

1.

The hammer connected with Colin MacGregor's head with a satisfying crunch that splintered his skull into fragments beneath the skin. The first smash stunned him, making him sway on his feet. The second dropped him to his knees and broke the skin. A trickle of blood snaked its way down the side of his face. The third hit was the killer blow. The head of the hammer dug into brain. When it was pulled out, a splattering of gore dribbled to the floor and Colin fell onto his back. A split second later and his body started to convulse violently. The fourth blow, accompanied by a loud female scream, stopped the involuntary twitches. Another death. Another commercial break.

*

Perspiration, tight clothes, even soaps can cause feminine itching and burning. Vagisil medicated cream relieves external itching fast and soothes irritation. No wonder so many women trust it. Vagisil, the relief you need right where you need it.

*

Victoria Ann Ballard, Vicki to friends and viewers, didn't get to see the commercial break. She didn't even know it had happened. Her world wasn't big enough for commercial breaks and pleasant little intervals anymore. Her world - at least for the time being - was a lot, lot smaller: Confined to this room and whatever lay beyond the door with the note attached.

To proceed, one of you must die.

Vicki dropped the hammer to the floor. It landed with a loud thud which splashed a little more gore across the way. Her eyes were fixed on the dead body of the man she had awoken with. The man she didn't know. The man she'd never know. Someone's son, someone's partner, someone's father, her victim.

Across the room, the large heavy metal door - previously locked - emitted a loud click before it slowly opened. Vicki turned to the door and took a step towards it, hopeful that freedom was on the other side. She stopped. She had no idea how she had come to be in this room, just as she had no idea who the man she had killed was - other than the name he had given her: Colin MacGregor, a name she would never be able to forget. She took another step towards the door and - for a second time - hesitated. There was no guarantee that the open door led back to the life she had been snatched from. Whoever put her here - would they really just let her go after forcing her to kill someone? A creeping sense of unease returned, similar to the way she had felt when she had first seen the note on the door prompting the occupants to kill one another for their freedom. A joke, she thought at first. Until, that is, she saw the look on Colin's face. A look which suggested he hadn't seen it as a joke and - instead - was taking it very seriously. *Don't think about him. You both could have talked it through and tried to find another way. What happened was because of him. He made it happen.* Another gripe in her stomach. What if this was just the start of something worse? What if - beyond the door - there was more of the same? Cruel tasks to complete and fight her way through before - finally - the freedom that was promised… Freedom back to her own life or freedom from the room? The million dollar question.

Can't stay here forever.

With no further hesitation she bent down and picked up the hammer for a second time. Even if it wasn't needed beyond that door, it made sense to keep hold of it for now.

Hammer in hand, she took another step closer to the door.

'Hello? Is anyone out there?'

There wasn't any *one* person. According to last week's viewing figures there were 1.4 million people out there. All eyes on her. All eyes curious to see just how far she would get in *The Game*. Some people willing her to make it the whole way and others hoping she didn't get far at all - already angry that she'd survived this long with their own bets having been placed upon what had turned out to be nothing more than another fresh corpse for the ratings.

The bets had been placed and the books temporarily closed.

2.

Shane Ryder turned his back on the large screen in centre position of the stage he owned. On the screen, a live-feed of what was happening in the warehouse as Vicki edged ever closer to the newly opened door.

With his back to the display, Shane now faced the live studio audience as a multitude of cameras captured his movements for the audience watching from home. His expression was one of pure joy, his gestures over the top and wild - the actions of an excited man.

'Well - who of you had voted against Vicki then? I bet you're kicking yourselves now, right? But then, you should realise now that things can go either way in this game. Nothing is guaranteed!' He turned to the camera, 'I'm sure you all remember the midget we had on the show a few weeks ago?'

The people watching from home were treated to a playback of the situation Shane was referring to. Violent images as a midget gripped tightly on to another man's neck, biting hard through the skin and piercing the main artery as the victim tried to shake him free. It was a playback Frank Meyer didn't need to see. Like many other people sitting there, watching, he had bet a lot of money against the midget. Betting on a six foot hulk of a man over a fucking midget seemed like the logical choice. At home, the playback cut back to the studio feed.

'But as we always say, you never know how people are going to react in these situations. The smallest people can fight the hardest and the biggest people can surprise you by rolling over and playing dead!' He paused a moment. 'But that's what makes it so damned exciting!' He yelled, 'RIGHT?'

The studio audience, prompted by an overhead sign, cheered and clapped. Shane gesticulated to quieten them down.

'Ssh! Ssh! Okay, okay... I get it... You're all excited... But... we have a question... Just how far is this little lady going to get? Will she die in the warehouse or will she get out and meet us here ready to choose a prize she will *truly* love?' He paused a moment to let that sink in. 'Let's get back to the action!'

Prompted again, the audience cheered.

Before the action, though, for the people at home - another commercial break.

*

Every year, thousands of people are forced to drink dirty water...

3.

On the other side of the metal door was a long corridor with only one door at the far end. There was an overhead light, constantly flickering on and off. Enough to give a person a headache. The floor, underfoot, was mostly wooden - clear of litter despite a coating of thick dust.

'Hello?' Vicki called out - oblivious to the cameras built into the wall - watching her through the smallest of peep-holes. An unseen audience. Squinting through the flickering of the light - there seemed to be some kind of flap built into the door. A letterbox but smaller than one you would find on a normal door. Next to the door, something sticking out - like, she squinted harder, a box? Nervously - half-expecting someone to leap out at her, although from where she couldn't say - Vicki walked towards the far door. The only sounds being the buzz of the overhead light, her light footsteps upon the wooden slats and the heavy thud of her heartbeat above all else.

Even though she knew there would be no answer, she called out again, 'Hello? Is anyone there?' The sound of her own voice, breaking the silence, somehow making the situation *a little* better than the near silence. 'Anyone?' Unsurprisingly there was no answer. Not audible to her at least. At home, watching from the comfort of their living rooms, people were answering her - openly mocking her, teasing her shaking voice and laughing at how petrified she looked even with Colin's gore splattered on her otherwise pretty face.

The viewers, both at home and in the studio, had heard it all before: People calling out for help, people asking if anyone was there and even people ranting and raving - screaming obscenities over and over again in the hope their abductor(s) could hear them. The viewers loved it all but - mostly - when the contestants had a full-on melt down, something which usually occurred when they realised they were being watched as part of the show.

'What the fuck is this? YOU SICK FUCKS!'

On the door was another laminated note that caught Vicki's eye before the perplex box attached to the wall, and the knife within it. The knife's blade crusted in dried blood from previous contestants who'd made it this far. The note read: *A thumb or a finger to proceed.* Vicki looked at the box, her heart pounding harder as she realised what was being asked of her.

Tucking the hammer between her belt and slim-fit jeans, she lifted the lid of the perplex box and reached in for the knife. A look over her shoulder, an uneasy feeling that she was being watched from somewhere.

Is this for real? A rhetorical question given the fact she'd already been forced to kill someone in order to save herself. If this wasn't for real than someone would have interrupted them before either one even had a hold of the hammer. Or - failing that - the hammer itself would have been nothing but a realistic-looking prop. This was real all right. A sick game of a sick mind.

Vicki turned her attention to the door. A sudden thought that - maybe - she'd be able to use the knife to pick a lock. She wouldn't know where to start but if there was a chance she could do it - it was a chance she would have to take… Her heart sunk, having momentarily felt hopeful of finding another way out of the situation. There was no lock on the door. There was just that small letterbox-like flap, the bottom of it coated in dried blood that had - once upon a time - trickled its way down the door having been smeared there by someone (she presumed) feeding the severed digit through. *Other people had done this? How far had they got?*

Vicki tried to wedge the knife between door and doorway but the gap wasn't big enough to get the blade between. She screamed out loud as the slow realisation of what she had to do continued to sink in. She wasn't the only one to try various different routes of escape. And - just as she hadn't been the only one to try - she wouldn't be the only one to fail either. There was one way out and that was through a simple choice. Or rather, a simple choice on paper. In reality, there was nothing simple about it whatsoever.

Defeated, she slid her back down the wall until she was sitting on the floor. Head hung low, she started to weep. Tears for missing her life, tears for the man she had killed and tears for what needed to be done. She also hadn't been the first to cry.

*

For hands that do dishes, Fairy Liquid...

4.

The large screen displayed Vicki's picture: A photo stolen from the semi-detached cottage she shared with her husband, Martin, in their family home in a village in Huddersfield. It was the couple on their wedding day and showed Vicki to be both elegant and beautiful - a far cry from the way she now looked, having been forced into her current predicament: Tired, weary, broken.

'Vicki has been a life long Huddersfield Town fan! A woman who loves her football - and her football players! Question is though,' Shane said - letting the audience get to know a little more about the surviving contestant, 'can she explain what the off-side rule is?' The audience laughed.

'Doubt it,' said one lone person, watching from their living room.

'The man on the right - a handsome fellow, don't you think? - her husband Martin! They went to Brooksbank School - in Elland of all places - together back when they were younger. When Martin was aged fourteen (or, he thinks, fifteen) he asked young Victoria out on a date - on Valentine's Day, no less!'

Awwwwwwwww, from the audience.

'Using money he had earned from his paper-round, he bought her a giant card and a *real red rose*! And people say romance is dead.'

Laughter.

'That - of course - did not stop our lady here turning him down in favour of Barry 'Bow-Legged' Jenkinson! Still - it wasn't meant to be and twenty years later our couple here found themselves again through the joys of Facebook. They were married on December 30th, 2011 and the rest, they say, is history in the making!'

Applause.

'The question is - though - can she find her true love again? Will the two be reacquainted or will she starve to death in that corridor...' The large television screen comes back to Vicki sitting on the floor of the hallway with the knife still in hand. 'Stay tuned to find out! We'll be right back after a word from our sponsors!'

The audience was prompted to clap again as Shane walked off stage towards the make-up artist.

'Great show!' Helena gushed as Shane took his seat in front of her - tools of her trade by her side.

'You expect anything less?'

'Of course not. I'm just saying...'

'Less *saying* more dabbing...'

'Yes. Sorry.' Helena - a huge fan, not of the show but of Shane himself, covered Shane's shoulders with a protective sheet and started applying more make-up on her favourite host. Various products designed to stop the glare of the studio lights reflecting from his skin. Every time she had to work with him, she always tried to start a conversation. And every time, he shut that shit down. Known for his bad boy behaviour, off-screen, he didn't spend his time fucking the help. He only dallied with those who could help take his career to the next level unless he was *really* desperate. He'd even lost count of the number of female studio executives he'd fucked over the years for the promise of *prime time*. Now he was working on this show for the Dark Internet. Broadcast to millions through word of mouth and streamed via satellite direct to their homes for a modest subscription. It might not have been a normal prime-time channel but the money offered - more than any studio could offer him... 'We're done,' Helena said - removing the sheet from around his neck. He stood up and straightened his suit by giving it a short, sharp tug. Without so much as a thank you, he walked back onto the stage ready to pick up from where he'd left off. He stopped in his tracks and turned back to Helena. 'Meet me in the dressing room for the third act.'

Helena's face couldn't contain the shock of being asked to his dressing room, nor could it hide the excitement. A grin stretched from ear to ear as Shane continued back to the stage.

'She fucking moved yet?' he asked knowing his producers could hear him via the ear-piece.

Still sitting there but definitely threatening to do it.

Shane sighed heavily as he thought of what else to talk about. He had always said this segment was a problem given the fact that there was no *real* sense of urgency. Having someone come at you, with the aim of killing you, forces you to act. Having someone sit in a hallway with the instruction to remove their own finger - of course they wouldn't do it immediately. It's not in a person's nature to be able to do that to themselves. Sure, the only way to get out was by complying but it still didn't mean they had to do it there and then. Yet if the hallway had walls that started to move inwards - threatening to crush the person making the choice - *then* there would have been a sense of urgency that would, undoubtedly, have forced them to act faster. This - Shane had often said - would have effectively killed the dead air that the viewers were forced to watch, preventing the possibility that they would start channel hopping in search of something more exciting.

'You know what I'm thinking, right?' he said out loud, knowing the producers would, once again, pick it up.

We'll look into it for the third season. The voice in his ear warned him they were due back on air within 3, 2….

'And welcome back! You'll be pleased to know you didn't miss any of the fun stuff whilst you were away and - better yet - it looks as though you've come back just at the right time!'

Victoria screamed on the giant screen behind him as she held out her hand - choosing which finger she could best afford to lose. The audience in the studio cheered at the thought of the impending bloodshed. More Gore. More Ratings.

5.

Vicki pressed her left hand down against the wooden flooring with her fingers outstretched. In her right hand, she gripped the dirty knife. Her mind wasn't concerned about the dried blood on there and neither was it concerned with the risk of infection and blood loss. Now it was fully focused on her family: Reece, her twenty-two year old son, and Rachael her twenty-one year old daughter. Of course Martin, her husband. Even Luke, the family dog - a black springer / Labrador cross. All of them were in the forefront of her mind causing her eyes to well up at the thought of possibly never seeing them again. *You will see them again, you just need to do this...*

She held the blade over her thumb at first before moving it to her little pinky. It might not be comfortable to use the hand without a little finger but it would still be easier to use it then if it were missing a thumb... She paused a moment. *Is that right?* Of course it was.

Unbeknownst to Vicki, a camera overhead zoomed in on her hand ready to give the viewers the gore they so desperately desired. The people, both at home and in the studio audience, leaned forward in their chairs practically chomping at the bit. First the hammer and now this...

Vicki pulled the blade away and suddenly screamed seemingly unable to go through with it as her mind started imagining the pain she'd feel. Yet, there was no choice. She needed to do this. She had to grit her teeth and just get it done. The sooner it was done, the sooner the door would open and she would be one step closer to the freedom offered by the initial note. The note. *What the fuck is all of this?*

She put the blade back against her little finger and pressed down. The pain was instant even though she hadn't even made a cut yet. She gritted her teeth and pulled the blade back with the metal, serrated teeth catching the skin and ripping it open. Unable to stay quiet she screamed as she pressed harder and pushed the blade forward as the blood started to flow freely... First forward and then back - a sawing motion. Her screaming intensified as the teeth scraped across bone, a shaky vibration through her body.

As word got around - with friends sharing the link to the live-feed - the viewing figures continued to steadily increase.

Dude, what the fuck is this?

                                      Awesome, isn't it? Keep watching.

Is this for real?

                            I shit you not, she just bashed some guy's head in.

What?

                              With a fucking hammer. It's insane.

Why the fuck is she cutting her own finger off?

                        She has to put it through the letterbox to get the door open.

Where the fuck did you find this?

                              Can't remember. You not a fan then?

Didn't say that LOL She get naked at all?

                              Last time there was a room with...

                        Actually I don't want to ruin it. Keep watching !

She is pretty fit. Even with one finger missing lmao

New viewers and new members signing up for when the shows were to air next.

Vicki pressed harder, struggling to cut through the hard bone although - with a sawing motion - she was making *some* progress despite the fact that the world around her was spinning. With sweat covering her skin, shimmering in the flickering light whenever it was "on", she struggled to keep conscious and stop from vomiting. *Don't vomit on the wound.*

The pool of blood beneath her hand was seeping into the wood, increasing the staining where it had already been stained by previous contestants who had - unwittingly - chosen the same spot to perform the task asked of them. They weren't on Victoria's mind though: Neither them nor the dirty blade possibly contaminating her own blood with whatever they could have been carrying through their veins. Her mind was still focused solely on her family as she continued to try and push through the pain to just get it done.

Suddenly the blade cut through the remaining bone and skin before it slammed down onto the wood beneath. The finger rolled a centimetre or two before coming to a rest. This lifeless digit that had once been a part of her. Horrified with what she had done, she dropped the knife and raised her bad hand up towards her face to get a closer look. The blood was leaking from the fresh wound, running down her hand as the pain continued to throb at the point of cut. Her whole hand... *Body...* Shaking violently as shock tried to set in. *Not done yet, girl.*

With her good hand she scrambled for her disconnected finger. She picked it up and - desperate to go home - posted it through the letterbox. The door's lock clicked across and - slowly - the door creaked open. No sunlight came through though. On the other side was just darkness. She clambered to her feet and - using the wall to balance herself and holding her bad hand against her body - she pushed through into the next room.

Reece.

Rachael.

Martin.

Mum and dad…

Luke…

Reece.

Rachael.

Martin.

Mum and dad.

Luke.

Reece….

Names, over and over again, to keep her going. Keep her strong.

Standing in the blackness of the next room, straining to see, the door behind her suddenly slammed shut. She jumped and span around but was now completely blind to where she was and what was to happen.

'Hello?'

The light flickered on. A few feet away from her was a pillar with a glass jar on the top of it at a thirty degree angle. Fairly close to this - hanging from the ceiling - was a metal cuff. A note, on the far door, had the instruction; *Put your good hand in the restraint.* It was a note ignored at first as Vicki looked around the room in the hope she would see something that meant she wouldn't have to do as she was told. A way out that they had missed perhaps. Whoever *they* were. Other than the jar, on the pillar, there was nothing else on the floor. There were five doors. One in front of her which, she presumed, was the exit. A door on each wall to the side of her and - obviously - the one she had just come from, on the back of which was another perplex box that was filled with various severed fingers.

Nothing else. Just that damned note. *Put your good hand in the restraint.*

Still unaware that she was being watched, she reached up with her bad hand - still throbbing in pain and still bleeding. She put it in the restraint, expecting it to clamp shut around her wrist but - nothing happened.

'Hello?' she called out.

*

The little boy - sitting on the toilet - laughed as the golden retriever puppy ran from the room with the end of the toilet roll in its mouth. The toilet roll spinning on the holder as each and every sheet was pulled away in one long string. As the last of the toilet paper slipped from the cardboard tube, the boy went to grab it only to miss. His laughter stopped as he realised he was stuck.

'Mum!' he called out in the hope she would hear.

The puppy sat on the stairs, surrounded by toilet paper, looking cute and innocent.

A voiceover: 'Soft and long. Andrex.'

6.

'Viewers of a sensitive nature should turn away now, possibly for the next couple of hours as the next game can take some time to finish…' Shane said in a serious tone the moment the feed cut back to him in the studio. His eyes were fixed to camera one, unblinking. 'Still here? Of course you are.' A sudden smile spread across his mouth. 'Why? Because you're not fucking pussies, that's why!' He turned to the screen behind him. Vicki was still standing in the centre of the room with her bad hand in the restraint hanging from the ceiling. He tutted. 'How stupid does she think we are?' And - then - he shrugged. 'We'll all just stand here until she gets it right then!' Mercifully for him, knowing how much he hated dead air, it didn't take long for Vicki to finally realise that she was most likely being watched. As a result, she pulled her bad hand back close to her body and put her good one in the restraint. It immediately locked around her wrist, trapping her in place. 'Whoops!' Shane laughed. 'Looks like we might have a quick learner here…' Inside he was relieved. This wasn't a quick segment of the show but it was sick enough to keep the sick fuckers glued to the proceedings and - more importantly - sick enough to ensure they kept sharing the link with like-minded friends. The viewing figures were about to go through the roof. He turned back to the audience and repeated, 'Seriously though, if you're easily offended - now would be a good time to fuck off.'

The audience - unprompted - laughed.

He shrugged. 'Your choice, kids.' He turned back to the screen and shouted, 'Bring on the Specials!' The audience - some of whom had sat in the same seats for other shows having spent thousands on what could be described as a Season Ticket - cheered. Of those who knew what was coming - some cheered because they got off on watching and others, the crueller members of the group, just found the whole thing hilarious. Shane walked off stage. It made for good viewing but not for him. Knowing how long this segment could take - he preferred to take the time out back with a cold drink and - if the opportunity presented itself - a blow job. The audience didn't care that he had left them to watch the screen. They knew he'd be back - centre stage - when he was needed.

*

Vicki pulled against the restraint even though she knew her efforts were pointless. Whoever had put it there, directing her to use it, wouldn't have done so had it been easy to break away. Even so, she pulled at it again. Her thought process suggesting that it could have started off as being secure but - over time - been weakened from the other people who'd been forced to play this "game". There was a possibility that the restraint wasn't checked after each person had come free from it. She tugged again but still no movement. Suddenly a noise from beyond the room startled her. She froze - trying to follow the sounds from behind the wall with her eyes. *What is that?* It sounded like people muttering - not that she could make out the words. It sounded like the shuffling of feet on wooden floors. People banging against the walls.

Two of the four doors in the room clicked open. Not the exit and nor the one she had come from but - instead - the other two which faced opposite each other. Vicki screamed as four men stumbled in through each doorway - their arms bound by a straight jacket with an electronic mechanism attached that glowed red for *locked.* Other than the straight jacket they were completely naked - all of them sporting proud erections. From their mouths, dribble dripped freely as Vicki came to realise that not all was okay with these men: The words they muttered nothing more than gibberish.

On one of the men's jacket - fastened over the lock - was another note. *With enough semen collected, the door will open and the restraint will loosen.* That heavy sickness feeling swirled in the pit of Vicki's stomach again as it dawned on her what she was being asked to do - a feeling which intensified as the men started crowding her, each trying to touch her, kiss her, lick her with only the *touching* stopped thanks to the straight-jackets keeping their hands locked to their own bodies.

The locks on the jackets clicked from red to green.

At home - the audience went crazy as the straight-jackets were shaken off and the once-tied hands became free to grab and pull. Victoria screamed as the first set grabbed her hair.

7.

Shane's hard cock slid into Helena's mouth, guided by her hand. Her lips wrapped around his shaft: Firm yet soft. Her right hand cupped around his balls and her left hand on the base of his penis. With one hand on the top of her head, helping to guide her movement, he turned his attention to the flatscreen television hanging on the wall.

'What do you think makes them grab at her?' he asked, watching the mentally-stunted men grab at Victoria. Looking at the screen, she was still screaming as she tried to push them away with her one free hand. Shane and Helena couldn't hear the screams. Classical music pumped into his dressing room, thanks to the iPod plugged into the sound system. For much of the audience - the screams were a part of the show. For Shane though, they were a distraction first and now an annoyance. Once you'd heard one person scream, you had heard them all. Helena didn't answer his question. With his hand holding the back of her head, she carried on sliding her lips up and down his shaft - wetting it with her warm saliva - as he continued, 'Do you think they want to hurt her? Or maybe they're trying to get her free? A little part of their broken minds recognising that she is in trouble, perhaps?' He paused a moment and sighed as Helena's sucking started to pay off and the pleasure started to hit home. 'Maybe they recognise what she is - a woman - and there's a sexual desire there to touch her… This woman, so different from them? That could be it?' He turned away from the screen to look down at his companion, for however long it took her to get his cum in her mouth and down her throat. Sensing his look, she glanced up to him with blue eyes so full of mischief.

Shane looked back at the television as Helena closed her eyes. In her own mind she thought of this as the appetiser. She'd suck him for a while, getting her own pussy nice and wet in the process such was the satisfaction of having his dick in her mouth. Then she would kick off her black satin panties and hitch up the short skirt she wore. He would hold her close as she slid her cunt down over his throbbing member and there she'd ride until she felt his hot cum spurt up inside her as he bit down on her nipples. The reality was far different. This was as much as he would ever allow someone like Helena. A shot in the mouth of his heavy load and, for that, she should be thankful.

On-screen Vicki pushed another of the men away from her. Her mouth open, clearly she was screaming again. Shane wondered whether it was because she was scared of the men - and trying to scare them by being overly loud - or whether it was because of the pain her hand must have been in, amplified each time she pushed someone away.

One of the men grabbed her from behind and slid his hands down the front of her jeans. She screamed again as she tried to wriggle from his grip but already his dirty fingers were pushing up inside her cunt - the nails scratching the internal wall as they delved deeper despite the dryness.

'That's good,' Shane sighed as Helena's tongue flicked the sensitive head of his dick. Pleasure for him, pain for Victoria as she tried to break free from the man's wandering fingers. 'Play with my balls,' he said. Helena didn't need asking twice. She continued caressing his testicles; gentle yet firm with a determination to get him off. A need and desire to taste the salty cum his testicles held. She pulled her mouth from his cock and started stroking up and down the length of his shaft - her eyes fixed on his face which, in turn, was fixed upon the screen as he watched

Victoria. She had gotten the message and was trying to wank off the men in the room with her. As three of them tugged at her clothes, tearing them here and there - grabbing flesh at every opportunity, she frantically wanked the fourth man - his throbbing erection aimed towards the glass jar as his hands also tried to grab for her.

Drowned out by the classical music playing in Shane's dressing room, Victoria was speaking. Through tears - both fear and pain - she was telling the men that she would get to them all and it would be so much easier if they would line up for her as opposed to continuing to grab at her. She told them, hiding disgust in her tone, that she wanted each of them to ejaculate for her - a wish that they could understand her words and do it for themselves. The only problem was, even if they could, they would most likely aim to put it in - or on - her, as opposed to the jar that was waiting to be filled.

Shane watched the pained grimace on her face intently as she wrapped her remaining hands around the man's dick. Her own blood now a lubricant for his enhanced pleasure. Despite the missing digit, she was doing well with her momentum and - surprisingly - her grip.

As Helena continued wanking - up and down, up and down, up and down - Shane imagined what it would be like to get the bloody hand job from Vicki... The feeling of less fingers around his shaft, the warmth of the blood... The heavy breathing of someone fearing for their life... The *smell* of her fear...

Shane's whole body twitched. Helena - still stroking - quickly positioned her mouth over the end of his shaft and not a moment too soon. A second later and her mouth was filled with his hot semen. Satisfied, she pulled away and wiped the residue spunk and dribble from around her mouth with the back of her hand. He still wasn't paying her any attention as she gulped it down. His eyes - and thoughts - still fixed on the show.

The first of the men ejaculated.

'Get out,' Shane said coldly. He was done with her. Helena had known all along she was being used and hadn't cared but - even so - the tone of his voice hurt. She got up, quickly checked her appearance in the mirror's reflection, and left the room. She closed the door behind her and - on screen - Vicki tried to get a second man in front of the jar. The playback cut to more ads.

Fucking commercials.

End of Part One

THE GAME

Broadcast across the world, transmitted onto the Internet via private satellites, The Game took various people from around the world and forced them to complete sadistic tasks in order for them to both win their freedom and a prize that they would truly love. Word of mouth was what got the show the audience it had today and whilst it would be easy for the footage to be tracked and the people behind the show to be brought to justice, it was left to stream. Why? Money. The company who owned The Game paid millions into most countries' governments and the countries it gave nothing to - well, they were the ones who couldn't do anything to have the show shut up. The poor countries which were left to rot in their own urban decay. But where did the money come from? Memberships and subscriptions for people to view the footage. Each person who followed the link - sent via friends - had a fifteen minute teaser before the footage cut out and they were prompted for payment. Unlike other sites that gave various options as to timeframes, this only had one choice: People had to pay monthly.

At 29.99 a month, human life is cheap - more so when you consider the subscribers also had the chance to win prizes for their loyal membership. The longer they stayed subscribed, the higher the chance they would win something big - such as a car, holiday or other luxury item they might not usually be able to afford for themselves. Then, of course, there were the Season Ticket upgrades for people who either wished to purchase them up front or who stayed subscribed for a year. This particular ticket giving them a special pass meaning - if they were close enough - they could go to one of the studio audience sessions. Each country hosting its own audience session to ensure it was fair for all.

The contestants had come from the streets initially. Homeless people who were snatched or bribed to take part - the latter not fully understanding the implications of signing up to become a star. They just heard the figure of the money offered and had dreams of future stardom. After all, any old pillock can forge a career once they've gone on at least one reality television program. You just had to look in the trashy magazines to know that much although that wasn't as depressing as those who simply released a fuck-video of themselves to get to the big-time…

After a while the show-runners moved away from the homeless people. For one, since starting, the shows had helped clean the streets of many vagrants and - for another - the viewers seemed less interested than when they watched the episode with the "normal" person. A woman from the posh part of the town that had been snatched from her day to day life when they could find no one else to play with… Like the homeless men before her, they put this woman through Hell and she fought even harder than any of the others before. Why? A homeless man has little to lose but a lot to gain. A "real" person had something to gain but too much to lose. This woman wanted her life back and - evidently - would do anything to get it back.

She had died in the final room - a victim of shock from wounds suffered in the first fight she had encountered.

Knowing how popular the show was, money also came to the company in the form of sponsorship. Various companies paying through the nose to have their commercials shown during the unnecessary breaks. Each ad costing almost treble what a normal advert would have cost on a standard television network. The companies didn't care though. They knew this was where the audience was and - even though these people were getting off on watching others suffer - they didn't care *who* their potential buyers ended up being. To them - money was money no matter who was spending it.

The Game was currently on its third season. Each season saw at least ten contestants play. Less than half of them survived. Of those who perished, the families complained and tried to seek justice against those who murdered them yet each case was dismissed. The world was - and is - a cruel place and money had spoken.

The games would continue.

*

Victoria Ballard had been used to hearing things in the family home, even when the rest of the family was out and the dog asleep in front of the fire. Before they moved in, the house had been empty and Martin and Victoria often discussed the idea that the previous owner had died in one of the rooms. *Natural causes.* Even so, Vicki said it was the spirit of a young girl she felt living there with them. When she heard a creak, or a door slam, and knew the house to be empty - she simply put it down to the little girl moving around.

Naturally, when she walked into the kitchen and saw the masked men by the open back door - she screamed. She fell to the floor as a heavy gloved fist smashed her in the face. Dazed, confused and scared - she heard a gunshot ring out. Still seeing stars, she turned her head to the side just in time to see the family dog drop to the floor. She screamed again. Moments later, another punch, and all was silent.

'Why'd you shoot the dog, asshole?'

'You want that thing biting you?'

'It's hardly a fucking Pitbull!'

'Whatever. Fucking thing would be barking all afternoon anyway. You want the rest of the family to be alerted when they come home?' Pause. 'No, didn't think so. Now get her in the fucking van and quit your bitching.'

PART TWO

8.

Creamy sperm slowly trickled down the side of the jar to join the rest of the semen pooling there. The door opposite Victoria's entry point clicked open, as did the restraint holding her good hand above her head. The moment it released her, she dropped to the floor despite the men still pawing at her. Quickly, she jumped up and pushed them away - kicking one of the touchy men straight in the testicles.

All the men - watching from both studio and their homes - crossed their legs and let out a collective groan of discomfort as they imagined the instant stomach ache. The watching women, on the other hand, laughed and cheered for Vicki. This was the one room they hated above all others - at least, when the contestant was a woman. When the contestant had been a man, forced to do as Vicki had just done, they couldn't help but laugh. Some of them even found the gusset of their panties moisten at the sight of a man stroking another.

Desperate to get away from the men, Victoria ran through to the next room without stopping long enough to collect the knife and hammer from where they had dropped to the floor. Without stopping, she ran through the room to the next door - locked shut, as usual, with a note attached. Her eyes fixed to not the note but what was on a small ledge close-by: A handgun.

The note: *Four bullets. Four Spastics. End them.*

As the first of the men entered the room - hands flailing in her direction as though desperate to continue grabbing at her - Victoria ran over to the gun. She picked it up and noticed another note beneath where it had laid: *It's ready. All you have to do is point and click.*

She turned back to the approaching men and raised the gun hoping it would be enough for them to rethink what they were doing and make a hasty retreat. The danger they were in didn't even register on their dumb faces. Trapped in a corner she fired once, twice, three... Four times. Each body crumpled to the floor like a sack of shit.

Despite there being no more immediate danger, Victoria didn't lower the gun as the barrel continued to smoke. Suddenly - making some people at home jump - she screamed and turned the barrel back against her own skull. A thought at the forefront of her mind telling her it would be easier just to give up and pull the trigger. Kill herself and end the suffering and - now - the guilt of having killed five people. The first note offered freedom but the cost was so high it was dawning on her that she would never truly be free. Even if she did get out, she would carry what she had gone through to her grave.

A little voice piped up in her head, *None of this is your fault.*

She lowered the gun from her head. Even if she did want to go through with it, the note was clear enough: *Four bullets. Four Spastics. End them.*

A few feet behind her, the next door opened. Slowly, Victoria turned to it. Given all that had been asked of her so far - what else could they put her through? What could possibly be worse?

Reluctantly, but with little choice, she approached the next door. With no warning both this door and the one she'd come from slammed shut. She jumped back. Confused, she turned around to see if she had missed something.

She had.

On the other door, visible now only that the door was closed: *Uh-uh-uh, you're not done yet. Drink the cum.* Upon reading the note, Vicki couldn't help but to gag at the mere thought of it.

*

Some of the audience members hid their eyes from the screen - too disgusted to watch the proceedings as Shane explained what the note had said, to those who had missed it.

'So for the next door to unlock - all she needs to do is drink up all that cum she helped make. Not a drop to be spilled!' he said with his usual enthusiasm. He continued, 'Shouldn't be too hard, should it? Of all the things asked - this has to be the easiest! Am I right? I mean - what girl doesn't like cum down the back of her throat?' He gave a sly glance off-stage to where Helena was sitting. She immediately felt her face flush with a paranoid thought that all of her colleagues knew what she had just done. To hide her embarrassment, she started rooting through her make-up chest as though looking for something previously lost.

Over the studio speakers from the live-feed - Victoria wretched as her guts twisted over what needed to be done. On-screen she already had the jar - twisted off from the stand - in her hand. Tilted it to an angle, the slime slid within - so thick that it wouldn't be a case of just pouring it down her throat. To get it down there, quickly at least, she'd need to spoon it down with her fingers. She gagged again as a little bile came up in the back of her throat. *Come this far, no choice but to go further.* A small part of her did wonder what would happen if she had refused though. Given the fact she had been forced to kill people already though - if only to save her own life in the first instance - she guessed the outcome probably wouldn't have been good. But, then, maybe that was the point? Maybe people only carried on because they felt the consequences wouldn't have been worth it? Maybe - by refusing - the *game* would just be over and whoever put her here would come and free her anyway? The little voice laughed. Her dog was dead. Five men were dead. Whoever put her here - they weren't about to just come and let her go if she refused to do something. That was painfully obvious - as was the fact she had little choice but to swallow this semen.

The audience reacted suitably as Victoria scooped the cum from the bottom of the jar and spooned it directly into her mouth. The thick muck, cold and congealed, caused her to gag for a third time as she swallowed it down as quickly as she could. Thick gravy. Still some in the jar. Without stopping to think about it, she quickly fingered that from jar to mouth too. Again, she gagged and - again - she swallowed. Some of the audience gagged too - not just as the sight of what Vicki was doing but the thought of having to do it themselves.

Shane laughed as someone in the audience threw up. There was always that one person. The screen cut to the next set of adverts as Vicki herself also started to throw up and the door in the next room - unlocked for a second time. *Click.*

9.

'How much do you love your children? Maybe you don't have any children? Well - what about your pets? The next room is killer. Literally. But - then - regular viewers will know that...' Shane mused, centre-stage. He was grinning from ear to ear. He knew the choice Victoria was going to make next. It was the same for all contestants who'd been in this position. They stood, locked in one room, with two windows that led to two different rooms. In one room was the family pet, the child or - in this case - the children: Reece and Rachael. Just as Vicki had been snatched away from her home, so had they. In the second of the rooms were a number of animals, if the other room had a family pet in it, or - as was the case now - ten toddlers, all of whom were happily playing with toys previously given to them by the monsters who'd gathered them here. Next to the window of each room was a single red button. All Vicki had to do to unlock the next door was press one of the buttons. 'If you were in this position,' Shane continued, 'what would *you* choose?'

*

Vicki screamed and started banging on the window separating her from her children. They could see her - and see she was screaming for them - but could hear nothing. Soundproof windows. She stopped hitting the window when she realised it was going to do her no good. Instead, she started looking for something to try and break through with.

'Wait... I have a hammer...' she tried calling through when she remembered the hammer she'd used earlier. As she turned back towards the door she had come from, it slammed shut and the lock clicked across. *No way out.* Only now, when she turned back into the room, did she notice the other room.

Ten children - aged two years old - were sitting in the room without an adult present. Each of them seemingly happy, playing with toy trucks (for the boys) and dolls (for the girls). One of the boys had willingly swapped his truck with one of the other girl's dolls.

'What is this?' Vicki muttered as she walked over to the room.

A young boy - blond hair and blue eyes - looked up and smiled at her through the window. He waved, oblivious to the tear that ran down Vicki's cheek. She looked away. Eyes immediately drawn to yet another note on the exit door: *To leave the room - press one of the buttons.*

Now she noticed the buttons.

Two large, red buttons. Neither of them giving a hint as to what they operated. Given how the rest of the rooms had been designed though, she knew that it wouldn't have been for anything good.

'What do they do?' she called out even though she knew she wouldn't get an answer. She waited. Hardly surprising - *no answer.* 'I can't press a button if I don't know what it does!' she called out again. Waiting for an answer she knew wouldn't come, she walked back over to the window separating her from Reece and Rachael. 'Are you both okay?' she asked. Cuts and bruises on their faces suggested they weren't completely fine but... *What these bastards done to them*?

Rachael was mouthing through the window that she loved Vicki.

'I love you too,' she answered - having read her lips. 'I love both of you.' With that, she turned away from them and hurried over to the other window. There was no way she was going to press a button which would put her children in danger. Without a second thought, she pressed the button on the wall next to the second room. Fearing what was to come, she took a step back from the window. Peering through, expecting the worse, her heart skipped a beat when a door opened within the toddlers' room. Masked men walked in.

'What are you doing?' Vicki asked, banging on the window. They answered with actions instead. Each man picked up one of the toddlers. Without so much of a glance through to Victoria's room, they turned and left. A second later, the door closed shut again. 'What...' Vicki stuttered. 'What are you doing?' she called out again.

In the studio Shane was laughing along with the majority of the audience. 'Maybe we ought to put an additional note in that room? Something, I don't know, to maybe warn the contestants what the buttons do? Something to think about, right?' He laughed. 'But then - we'd miss that classic look on their face when they realise what is happening if we did that...'

Vicki's face dropped as she turned to Reece and Rachael. The pair of them were standing by the window. The pair of them, clutching their throats. Their eyes bulging as a green gas willowed into the room via some previously unnoticed vents.

'No...' Panic started to set in. 'No! Please no!' Vicki hurried over to the window and started slamming it with her hands clenched into tight balls. 'Stop this! Please stop this!' she called out - hoping that whoever was watching would take pity and save her children. A foolish hope given all she had been put through so far. *Why would they take pity now?* 'Please... Why are you doing this?' She shouted through tears as she continued banging on the glass. Before her eyes, both children dropped to their knees as - slowly - their skin started to bubble and blister on any flesh exposed to the noxious gases. 'Please stop this!' she screamed again. Little blisters burst as pus seeped from the fresh wound. The skin, starting to dribble away from the bone beneath. Mozzarella cheese hanging off a pizza base. Clearly in pain, their mouths were open - desperately trying to form words as dark red blood spilled out from deep within, the toxins turning their insides into mush. Victoria wanted to turn away. She wanted to hide her eyes from the sight that would haunt her for the rest of her life, however long that may be, and yet she found she was unable. The last thing she wanted her children to see, no matter the pain they felt, was her: The woman who had raised them, the woman who loved them unconditionally...

'I'm sorry!' she shouted through the soundproof glass. Even if it weren't soundproof though, the words would have been lost. Their ear-drums had burst and ears themselves were leaking the same dark red that flowed from their mouths... And their eyes... Leaking down their faces and mixing into the wet flesh.

They weren't moving anymore. Both of them lying on the floor - still. Dead. Flesh still bubbling. Vicki screamed and dropped to her knees. The door to the right of Vicki clicked open. The next room waited. She didn't even glance across to it. A part of her had perished along with her children. What was the point in living now?

A voice - new to Victoria - came over a speaker system. It was Shane - talking from the comfort of his studio. The crowd watching him, hushed into silence before his microphone went live.

'You might feel like you can't go on. You might feel as though you don't want to, that you have nothing left to live for. But what about your mother and father?

What about your husband?' Shane paused a moment - giving Victoria's mind enough time to flash up images of those still living. 'Do you not want to see them again? Do you not want your husband... Your mother and father... Do you not want them to hold you and ease your grief. Tell you that, everything is going to be okay? They're waiting for you. Don't give up now. You've gone so far. You've accomplished so much. Do you really want all of that to be in vain?' He paused again. And - to dangle a carrot - he said, 'You're so close.' Shane turned the microphone-feed off, leaving Victoria alone once again. His words - prompted by a previous contestant refusing to go any further - would play their part. When he finished talking, they always continued, spurred on by the promise of seeing someone they loved again. The thought of their voice. The feel of their touch... The promise that, *it's not much further*. She knew there was a chance the stranger was lying about there not being that much further to go but she also realised there was a chance he could have been telling the truth too. Now was not the time to give up but - first - a commercial break.

10

The crowd cheered and clapped as the toddlers were walked onto the stage, carried by the people who had collected them from what could have been their death room. At least, to Vicki's knowledge, it could have been their death room. In truth, the buttons did nothing. The gas was controlled by the production team and - no matter which button the contestant pressed - the result would always be the same. The contestant's family pet or family member(s) would be the one(s) to perish.

'Of course we wouldn't hurt these darling children!' Shane said as he himself also clapped his hands together. 'These little munchkins are our future viewers!' he beamed. The applause petered out as the toddlers were taken directly from the stage area - back to where their parents were anxiously waiting at the back of the studio. When all was quiet, Shane continued, 'Two rooms left and then - so long as she survives - Victoria will get to choose a prize that she *truly loves*! Always a heart-warming part of the show to see them leave with something that means so much to them - especially after the hardships they've had to endure to get to that point... Question is though, *will* she make it? Does she have what it takes to get through the next rooms or - like so many before her - will she fall at the last hurdle?' He paused a moment to take a second to glance back at the screen. Vicki was still weeping for her dead children and had yet to go through the door to the next room. Shane chuckled to himself. This room always knocked people for six. He turned back to the audience, 'As always there is a little box under your seat with two buttons on it,' he told the crowd. 'A red button and a green button. If you think she will survive, press the green button! If you think she will die, hit the red.

As always one random person, who chooses the correct outcome, will win themselves ten thousand pounds!' The audience cheered again. 'So... Reach for those buttons and get voting!'

Each person in the audience leaned down and grabbed the box from under their seat. One red button, one green. They pressed the buttons with only a handful of people stopping any amount of time to give the outcome some serious thought. Most, instead, going on gut instinct only and pressing as soon as the box was in hand.

'Okay, if you haven't done it already... Be quick... You have five seconds left, four... Three... Two... One... Okay, voting *is* closed!' Shane clapped his hands together. 'Right - so let's see what you all think... *Will she survive* according to the viewers?' Shane turned to the screen behind him. The footage of Vicki cut to black and - a moment later - two lines came up on the screen: One red, one green. The red one was significantly longer than the green. The majority of the people thought she was going to die. In fairness, Shane felt the same too. She had done well to get this far but the last two rooms... *They were a fucking bitch.*

'Well,' Shane said, 'not much faith in Victoria, huh? Let's see if she can prove everyone wrong!' He laughed. 'Sorry it's too late to change your votes now but there's a few people in the audience who *do* have faith in her who are now desperately hoping she *can* prove the rest of the pessimistic bastards out there wrong. With so few of you believing she can survive, you fine folk have just cut your odds down massively on walking away with ten grand so... Best hope you're right and we're wrong!' The rest of the crowd, those who voted she would die, shifted in their seats nervously at the thought of even losing the *chance* to win the money. Ten grand was a lot. Not life-changing amount but - at the very least - a good vacation, or two.

*

Yet another charity commercial begging for viewers to give whatever they can afford on a monthly basis. Images showing malnourished children on their death beds. The viewers don't give a fuck. A dead child overseas is not their problem. The contestants dying for their viewing pleasure now - the families that suffer - also not their problem. This is the world we live in now.

*

Victoria staggered dazedly into the next room, as shock started to sink in. Her breathing had changed and she was practically hyperventilating. That teasing unknown voice promised an ending that was close and whilst it was a tempting carrot dangled before her - there was a sickness in her gut and a desire to die. How could she survive, living on having seen her children *melt* in front of her. She'd never forget the look in their eyes before their eyes turned to mush. The look on their faces as they melted beyond recognition… Before Vicki had a chance to see what the next room entailed, she dropped to the floor and vomited a yellow, acidic bile which stung the back of her throat. The taste… She threw up again.

'I've been where you are,' a woman spoke up causing Vicki to jump. She looked up. There, across the other side of the room, stood another woman. She was in her mid-thirties, dark hair and light green eyes, wearing a blue suit with a pencil skirt and white blouse. She looked good. Authoritative. 'I know how you are feeling.'

Vicki stood up and backed up against the wall as the door behind her clicked shut and the lock bolted across. She wasn't nervous about the way the woman looked, or even spoke. She looked smart and her tone was friendly. Sympathetic, almost. No, Vicki backed up because of what was in the woman's hand: A gun similar to the one Vicki had been forced to use earlier.

'You might feel as though you can't go on. I know because that's exactly how I felt but... I can give you an extra reason to make it out of here...'

Vicki swallowed her fear and tears down, if only for a moment, and asked, 'What are you talking about?'

11.

As the woman explained who she was and what she had to offer, the viewers at home were given a split screen to watch. On one side was the live feed of the two women and, on the other side, there was playback of this woman's time on the show. Imagery of her beating another woman to death, having to make a decision to press the red button for her baby boy or the red button for a room full of babies... *She made the same mistake as Victoria.* Then of course there was footage of her on her knees, spewing her guts up, as a man stood before her - just as she was standing before Victoria now.

'This gun has one bullet. You can use it to kill yourself and end your pain here - if you really think you don't want to live anymore - or you can get out of here and, when you do... You can use the bullet on the man who is running the show.' She paused a moment. 'Honestly speaking, though, this choice won't stop the show or mean other people won't have to go through this too... But... It will put an end to the life of the man who chose *you* and who put *your* family in this position. By putting them here, he effectively killed your children.' She emphasised, 'If you get out of here - you can have your revenge on him with no comeback. The call it the *free shot* policy. You get to kill the man who did this to you, you then get a prize and get your freedom. Once out, if you really can't live - or rather, don't want to live then...' The sentence didn't need finishing: Victoria still had the option to kill herself.

At home the screen stopped the playback short of showing the woman executing the (at the time) woman who had snatched her from her comfortable life to plunge her into this nightmare. At the time though, it had been a clean short straight between the woman's eyes. The bullet had burst through the rear of her skull with a fanfare of blood, brain and bone that had splattered the wall where she had sat. The show-runners were happy to relive the moments of past contestants going through hell but were never happy to share the results of the *free shot* outcome.

The *free shot* policy wasn't as crazy as it sounded for the person. They, like most of the audience watching, were gambling men and women. If the contestant made it to the end then - yes - there was a good chance they would cut their life short but if they didn't then the show-runner would walk away with a serious payday for having put on a good show. You bet your life and you win *big* if you bet right. And if they did die? Their families were still rewarded heavily for the loss they would suffer. It was a big gamble, yes, but - to a lot of people - it was worth it. Especially when it was rare that people made it right through to the end.

The woman held the gun out to Victoria who was dubious about taking it, unsure as to whether it was a trick or not.

'It's okay... I promise it's not a trap. They want you to have it because they want you to have an incentive to carry on going through the rooms.' She paused a moment as Vicki still struggled with the decision just to take the damned gun. 'Did you know you're being watched by millions around the world?'

'What?'

'They're all watching. Some in a studio and some in their home. People like you and me, we never knew about this *show* but there are millions of people out there who do know and they're all betting on you - as to whether you make it or die trying. Or, maybe you'll even just give up? Maybe you'll take the gun from me and put it to your head and end the broadcast here?' She carried on as Vicki digested all that was said. 'The show-runners obviously want you to carry on and that's why they are giving you this free shot policy. They're hoping your desire to kill the person who put you in this position will be enough to drive you on… It's a shitty, fucked-up show but that is what it is. Now it's down to you as to what you want to do. Do you want to kill yourself and end it all here? Do you want to kill the person who put you in this position and - ultimately - killed your children? Do you want to see your husband again? Or the rest of your family? Are you curious as to what prize they could offer you that would make *any* of this seem acceptable?' She stopped a moment. Silence. Dead air. She smiled. 'I'm not supposed to tell you what I walked away with but…' she paused a moment. This woman, this stranger, had her part to play: She had to come in and offer the gun for the free shot policy and that was it. If she tried to influence Victoria in anyway then she was under no illusion, she knew she wouldn't be allowed to leave. More than that, she was under no illusion that her other daughter would survive. She had lost one baby, she didn't want to lose another. Despite winning the game, she was still as much of a prisoner. She finished the sentence taking the safe route of doing as she had been instructed, 'I wasn't disappointed.' She said, 'Please, take the gun…'

Victoria came away from the wall and snatched the gun from the woman's hand before backing up again. She looked at it, unsure as to what to do. The woman hoped that Vicki would just turn the gun on herself and pull the trigger. A suicide now was the only way she was going to beat the show. With no contestant, there would be nothing to air and the season would be over for another year. Nothing more to air, no more commercial breaks. No more commercial breaks and less money than they had been hoping for. That was the way to hurt the show…

Financially. But of course Vicki wouldn't be thinking like that. She would be thinking about her dead daughter, her dead son… She would be thinking about putting this one bullet through the eye socket of the cunt who had done this to her family. Her judgement would be considerably clouded, just as her own judgement had been.

Victoria suddenly turned the gun towards the woman.

'What are you doing?' the woman asked.

'I could just kill you.' With her spare hand, Vicki wiped away a rogue tear that formed in the corner of her eye. 'How do I know any of what you said is true?'

The woman put her hands up. 'How do you know it isn't?' Panic evident in her voice, a desperation to get home to her daughter. A desperation…

The gunshot echoed throughout the room. The woman dropped down dead. The back of her head split open like a canoe leaking red as Vicki screamed towards her. After what had happened with the red button, she couldn't trust anything anymore. To her, everything was a trap. Everything was a part of this sick and twisted game… She screamed again as she turned the handgun to her own head. Another scream. She pulled the trigger. *Click*. Another scream.

'Fuck you! Fuck you!' she started calling again and again, looking around trying to see potential cameras filming her. They were there - the cameras - but too small to notice unless you knew what you were looking for. Another lesson learned from early seasons: The smaller the cameras, the less chance people would fuck with them. 'Fuck you! You're fucking cowards! Pathetic fucking cowards!' she screamed.

*

The studio was momentarily stunned into silence. The free shot policy had been in place ever since someone had frozen after killing someone dear to them. They had refused to do *anything* - even when they were staring down the barrel of a gun with their lives threatened. The new ruling was a way of getting even the most suicidal to push on through to the end in order to give the viewers the show they wanted. *This* was the first time the gun had been used to kill the messenger.

Suddenly the audience burst into applause and cheered at what they had witnessed. Shane himself even started to laugh.

From the comfort of her home, Colleen Cassidy leaned to her friend Christine Feldon and said, 'I don't expect they saw that one coming.'

'But surely that means she can't exercise her right to kill the producer at the end?' Christine pointed out. It was a fair point and it *did* mean she had lost her right to take another life for free. At this stage of the game though, it was fair to say Victoria didn't care.

Shane turned to his audience and asked, 'Okay - be honest - who saw that one coming? Anyone?' Pause. 'Anyone?'

'I did!' a lone voice called out.

'Fuck off did you!' Shane laughed again before getting serious. 'Question is,' he continued, 'what will she do next?' He was hopeful she would be driven enough to continue yet also feared she might now give up and play dead. If that was the case, if she did just stop, they'd have to send the cavalry in. Like the person from Season Three, she would then be given the choice: Continue or get a bullet between the eyes and everything done would have been for nothing. It was a choice that made for good drama as the viewers waited to see which route the contestant went down but it would be better if she continued without needing to be forced into it. Especially as - when in that position - most people just took the fucking bullet and were done with it. Always easier to have someone else pull the trigger that ends you than to take your own life.

Shane turned to the screen. Vicki walked through to the next, final room as the door unlocked.

The cleansing room.

12.

The note read: *Remove your clothes.*

Up above, a few feet in front of where she was standing, was a shower head. The rest of the room was blocked by a shower curtain which stretched from one side of the room to the other.

Small print on the note: *Wash away your sins.*

'I'm not stripping,' she said flatly. The thought of all those people at home watching, potentially getting off on seeing her naked. Knowing people were watching made *everything* worse. She said again, 'Did you hear me? I'm not stripping!' The door she entered the room from slammed shut. The lock clicked across. She shook her head. 'I'm still not doing it. Fuck you!'

Unbeknownst to Victoria, Shane was mocking her on the stage - imitating her voice yet making it sound more high-pitched and whiney than she was doing herself. The audience was lapping it up. Truth be told, it didn't matter if Victoria removed her clothes or not. Either way she was going to get a soaking with the overhead shower units. Her sins needed to be washed away one way or the other before she would be able to leave the game...

'Looks like we have a fighter!' Shane said joyfully. 'What say we wash her sins away with a shower!'

The audience cheered as a scantily clad blonde walked on stage in a thong-backed swimsuit. In her hands was a box and - on top of that - a big red button similar in style to the one Victoria pushed, condemning her children. She stopped next to Shane with a smile on her pretty face. This was the part of the show people loved: *Audience participation.*

Ignoring Victoria's screams of 'Fuck You' playing on the screen behind, Shane addressed the audience, 'You know what time it is? One of you gets to come down here and press this fucking button!' The audience cheered and clapped again. 'Normally this is done by random process but today is *not* a normal day!' He paused a moment as the audience hushed over. 'I believe we have an Edna Green in the audience… Am I right?'

'Over here!' someone called out from the audience. Shane followed the voice. A man - in his sixties - was standing up and pointing to a little old lady who was sitting next to him. 'This is her!' The woman was laughing and waving to Shane.

'Isn't it a special birthday today, Edna?' Shane asked, knowing full well what the answer was.

'She's 100 today!'

'One hundred years young!' Shane yelled enthusiastically as the audience applauded the woman for not being dead yet. In fairness to Edna, she looked good for her age. She walked unaided, saw clearly without the necessity for glasses. The only thing she did need were her hearing aids. 'Well, Edna, as it is your special day… Fuck the telegram from the Queen… We want *you* to come on down and press the button! What say you?' he yelled.

She responded by putting her thumbs up. The man sitting next to her, her son, cheered before he stooped down to help her up to her feet. She pushed him away, almost embarrassed that he had helped her. Shane saw and couldn't help but laugh, as did the blonde standing by his side. As Edna made her way down, the crowd cheered her along right up until the moment she was standing next to Shane and the beautiful woman with the big red button.

'I thought you would have at least got me a hunk,' Edna said as the audience quietened down. Everyone laughed.

'We'll know for next time, darling!'

'I'll hold you to that,' she said.

100 years old and still full of spunk with all faculties firing on all cylinders.

'So - you know what this button does?' Shane asked, moving the show along.

'I do.'

'And you're happy to press it?'

'I am!'

'Then - Edna - press away!'

Without hesitation, Edna pressed the button as the room burst into a cheer. In truth the button did fuck all, just as it had done nothing for Victoria. But that didn't matter. It was all about making believe it did something and - as soon as Edna pressed it - the production company backstage set off the showers over Victoria. Edna turned to watch what "her actions" had caused - via the big screen - as the shower-heads started spewing what everyone knew was *not* water. No longer needed, the blonde turned and started to walk off the stage - helped on her way with a playful slap of her arse from Shane. Later, if he felt the desire, he would cum in that and he couldn't help but to lick his lips at the thought of it as - on-screen - Victoria started screaming in agony.

Not water.

Acid.

*

The acidic substance caused Vicki's face to redden the moment it splashed down upon her skin. A burning sensation raged through her system causing her to scream out loud again as the red blotches started to crack and blister. Trying her best to cover her face with her hands, she staggered towards the curtain in the centre of the room. The moment she could, she lifted it from where it hung down to the floor and put it over her head to protect herself further. Here, she was safe. Although for how long, she didn't know. The burning skin and blinding pain still allowed a question to pass through the firing senses: *Could it get through her clothes and the curtain too*? Beyond the curtain more acid continued to pour from overhead showers - each of them unavoidable. The door - just as it had been for the other rooms - was locked shut with a note - protected by a glass frame - hung on it.

Find the key.

To the side, under the flow of the *water*, were five glass jars filled with clear liquid - no doubt the same as what was pouring from the ceiling. At the bottom of each jar - a lead box. Despite the panic, despite the pain… Vicki knew what she had to do. She had to reach into the jars and fish out the boxes. In one of the boxes, clearly there was a key for the lock on what she hoped was to be the last of the doors she'd face. Vicki pulled the curtain down off the hooks - nothing new to the people at home as each of the contestants before had done this as well. She wrapped herself in it - ensuring it covered her head too. Then, fully covered other than her face which she kept facing down to the floor, she made her way to the first jar with a speed in her movement brought about by a desperation to get out of the room and a fear of having the plastic of the curtain melt around her.

At the first jar, she adjusted the way she stood so that only one hand was needed to hold the curtain tight around her. A sneaking suspicion what was in the jar, she used her bad hand to reach in and quickly grab the lead box. The moment her skin touched the liquid, the liquid started to bubble and smoke and she couldn't help but to let out an ear-piercing scream. A searing pain immediately shot through her body, starting at her hand - which had already begun to blister from the acid - and going right through her. Even so, she grabbed the box and pulled it from the liquid. With her red-raw hand quivering, she opened the box up only to see that it contained just a note. Two words: *Try again.*

One jar down. Four to go. The acid continued to rain down upon her, occasionally splashing - and burning - whatever bit of skin wasn't presently covered by the curtain. She dropped the box and turned to the next jar and went to put her hand in - the faster she acted, the sooner it was over... She paused a moment. The briefest of seconds being all it took to realise there was a less painful way to proceed.

13.

There was nothing in the rules to dictate how contestants played the game. That was what kept everything fresh for the viewers. There were multiple ways to get through the game - as seen both when Victoria shot the messenger of the free hit policy and what she was doing now. Of course it was disappointing for the viewers when the contestants found a less painful way to proceed, as made clear with the studio audience's booing, but there was nothing Shane or the producers could do. If a contestant had the intelligence to proceed in a less painful manner previously unthought of by the show-runners, or contestants who'd played before, then *fair play*. However, what it did mean was, it wouldn't be possible to play the game in the same fashion for the *next* contestant...

Shane watched on - just as disappointed as the audience - as Vicki threw the lead box at the third glass jar. Just as the second glass had shattered, so did this one - spilling its acidic contents onto the already soaked floor. With the next box available to search, she grabbed it from the pedestal and opened it. Again, there was nothing inside. The truth was, there were no keys in any of the boxes. The game was just to watch the contestants search for it. When they got to the last, if they got that far, and they realised it was empty - that was when the door would click open with the sound of laughter played over the speakers.

'Hardly worth going through all of this, is it?' Shane muttered - fully aware that the producers could hear them from their booth situated beyond the studio audience. 'We're just going to have to buy more jars,' he correctly pointed out. It was this - the thought of spending unnecessary money - that caused the producers to open the door.

The door opened and Vicki dropped the shower curtain as she ran through it - head still low - straight into a pitch black room and - ultimately - a small metal cage. Before she had a chance to even realise where she was, the door behind her slammed shut - trapping her within the metal framework.

Feeling around in the pitch-black, she soon realised she was in a small cage. With hands on the cool bars, she screamed as - from a source unseen - water suddenly sprayed over her from all angles. This time it wasn't acid but normal water spray to wash away the burns, not that it stopped the pain she felt. Then, no sooner had the water jets started blasting her, they stopped. A second later and Vicki stumbled against the metal bars as the cage jolted upwards - seemingly rising on some unseen platform.

'What is this? What is happening?' she screamed into the darkness.

From up above a little ray of light suddenly beamed down as the ceiling above her started to open up. Looking up through the frame of the cage, Vicki could see that it wasn't a wide opening - just enough to let the cage pass through. Furthermore, she could see that where she was heading was brightly lit with a cool breeze coming down to where she shook in the cage. Above the metal clanking of the lift she could hear people clapping and whooping. *Is that for her?*

It didn't take long for the cage to reach where it was headed. It jolted to a stop in the middle of a stage. A man - cocky looking with an arrogant smile - sidled up next to her with a microphone in his hands as - in front of the pair of them - an audience continued to cheer and applaud. A good reception considering many had bet on her to perish.

'Congratulations! You're done!' Shane shouted as ticker tape started to float down from the ceiling after a mini-explosive set it all off. A half-arsed attempt at a fan-fare.

'Get me out of this fucking cage!' Vicki shouted over the cheers.

'Yeah, that's not going to happen anytime soon quietly,' Shane said.

The cage was a necessity to stop the winning contestants from going on a rampage when they got out of The Game. Although they were watched carefully whilst playing the game, there were no guarantees they couldn't have brought something out with them - something that could easily be used as a weapon. These people had been put through hell and there was every possibility that - given the opportunity - they would lash out violently against anyone, and everyone. Being the first person who got to speak to them, the cage was Shane's brainwave. Vicki would stay in it until long after the studio was cleared out. Then, and only then, would the automatic lock release and - as promised at the start of her personal nightmare - she would have earned her freedom.

Shane waved the audience into silence. They duly quietened down.

'Now,' he said to Vicki who was still screaming for her freedom, 'the bad news is… You opted to use your free-shot policy whilst in the game so - you've lost the chance to kill the director… Which I am sure he is thrilled about… But… All is not lost! You still beat the game! And what does that mean?' Shane turned to the audience for help.

They yelled, 'A prize you will truly love!'

'That's right,' Shane said excitedly, 'you still win a prize you will truly love!

And - we have two for you to choose from and we are dying to see which you will choose but, before we get to that...' He paused a moment. 'Did you know some of these good people bet that you would beat the game? Well, those who did bet correctly - they get a chance to win ten thousand pounds!' He turned to the audience. 'Who wants to win some money?'

The pretty blonde in the thong-backed costume came in from the side for a second time. Again, in her hands, a button ready to be pressed. She walked over to the cage and held the button towards Vicki.

'If you could just reach through the bars and press the button,' Shane prompted Victoria.

'Fuck you!' she hissed.

He shrugged. 'That's cool. We can press it ourselves...' Without waiting for a comeback from Vicki, not that he was going to get one, Shane leaned across to the button, presented by the assistant, and pressed it. Again, an act for show only. The producers controlled the lights that suddenly dimmed. They also controlled the spotlight which suddenly beamed down on one of the audience members: a young man who had voted in Victoria's favour. At least, that's who everyone else presumed him to be. The truth was, he was a plant - just like all the other people who had won before him. A family member of the show-runners put there to *win* the money that was (not) being offered.

Playing his part well, the man jumped up from his seat and punched the air.

'Well done, sir, you're now ten thousand pounds richer! Come on down and tell us your name!' Shane, like the other people behind the show, knew his name: Robert Duncan. Robert navigated his way to the stage where Shane was waiting to shake his hand.

'What's your name and where do you come from?' Shane asked - the stereotypical gameshow host.

'My name is Robert and I'm from London!'

The crowd cheered.

'So what are you going to spend the money on then?' Shane asked.

'You're fucking sick! All of you! You're sick!' Vicki screamed.

'Probably a new car, I guess...' Robert said. His eyes were wide with amazement. To those watching from the audience, and at home, he honestly looked as though he was star-struck. 'I haven't really thought about it... I never expected to win...'

'You know what I would spend that money on?' Shane asked.

'Fucking sick bastards!' Vicki screamed again.

'Coke and hookers!' Shane yelled. The audience cheered - half of them because it seemed like such a rock and roll thing to say and half of them because they knew he was being serious - especially given the fact it had been well documented in the press over the years, not that Shane gave a fuck. He turned back to Robert and said, 'But you're probably right - a car would be a more sensible idea...'

'Can I get a selfie?' Robert asked as he fished his phone from his pocket?

'What? Sure. Of course!' Shane grinned for the camera phone as Robert expertly lined the shot up to include the assistant, Shane, himself and - still screaming obscenities - Vicki. *Click - one for the album.* 'Thank you for this,' Robert said - again shaking Shane's hand as he slid the phone back into his pocket with his other hand.

'You're welcome...' Shane addressed the audience, 'Give it up for Robert who leaves here ten thousand pounds richer!' As Robert waved to the audience, heading back to his seat, the audience clapped and cheered. Shane waited for Robert to take his seat before he continued. 'All that we need to know now is,' he turned to Vicki, 'what prize you're going to choose!'

'Fuck you!' Vicki spat through the cage. With her body so dehydrated and energy levels low, the spit didn't get very far and certainly nowhere near where Shane was standing. He grinned at her pathetic attempt. 'Now, we promised you a prize you would truly love. Do you remember that?'

'Fuck you!' she hissed again. *Broken record.*

'Maybe but I'd have to insist you take a shower first.' The audience laughed. 'So… If you cast your eyes over there,' he pointed up to the ceiling on the far right of the stage, 'you will see what you can choose from…' Even though she had no intention of playing his sick games anymore, Vicki felt herself look up in the direction he had pointed. She screamed as the right side of the stage floor opened up revealing razor spikes beneath.

14.

Hanging from the ceiling were two more cages, similar to the one Vicki found herself in. In one of them was her husband, Martin. In the other were her parents - cramped together cuddling. Crying. Vicki screamed again as she quickly realised what she was having to do.

'You get to choose either cage. Whichever you choose - the contents of *that* particular one is what you will go home with today. So - do you choose the cage with your mum and dad or - maybe - you choose the one with your husband? *Decisions, decisions! Which will it be?'*

The crowd was going wild: Up on their feet, hands in the air clapping loudly as they continued to cheer - each of them wondering who Vicki would choose to take home.

'I must warn you though,' Shane said, 'whoever you don't take home... Well they get to stay here with us - *forever.'* He looked down to the blades just beneath the floor level on the right hand side of the stage. They were tainted red and some still had guts and flesh hanging off the very tips from where people had died before.

'Why are you doing this?' Vicki screamed.

Shane didn't answer. Instead, he had another warning for her. He continued, 'Let it be known though, if you refuse to make a choice - we will simply presume you don't want either of the prizes and, well, no sense us making a decision for you, hey? We will just open them both up and save you the hassle of having to take either.' He smiled at her.

The audience was shouting who they thought she should take home. Going by the majority, it appeared her husband was favourite to spare. That wasn't because they thought he was a nicer man though and deserved life over her parents. They just knew that, if Vicki saved him, they would get more bang for their buck with the parents falling to their deaths - impaled on the spikes. The catchphrase of the show: More Gore, More Ratings.

They wanted their gore and - in fairness to them - they hadn't had as much as some of the other shows had offered. Previous shows had violent clashes between contenders in the first room: Punches thrown and exchanged, biting, kicking, scratching, eyeballs being pulled from sockets. What did they have today? The bumbling idiot at the start grabbed the hammer and fucked up… She got it back and ended the fight quickly. Bloody, yes, but quick. To these people it was similar to what could be the best fuck they'd ever had. Their partner shows all the right signs of knowing what they're capable of but… They cum before they give you any satisfaction. A crude comparison but everything about this was crude.

The last room - with all the acid - was also usually good for some gore. Previous contestants had been so desperate to get out that they failed to see the route Vicki saw in smashing the glasses. These people just threw their hands down into the acid-filled jars until all skin was stripped from bone, left floating in puddles of pink on top of the acidic liquid. And the room with the spastics - even that had been a good source of the red stuff in the past with hands clawing at flesh with so much ferocity that they ripped through skin and grabbed handfuls of intestine and gut from within. The person, trapped by the cuff, standing there unable to do anything but cough up blood as they watched their insides pool out on the floor beneath them. On one show, a male contestant even had his dick ripped from his body in that room - again, literally torn away with nothing but fingers and nails separating it from body. "The Cock Rip" was often played back during quieter episodes that called for "The Best Bits" to be played over from previous shows in order to keep the viewers at home tuned in. There was no denying the audience this time round had a tamer show than the last - something that was already playing on Shane's mind.

As Shane waited on an answer from Vicki, as to who she would choose as her prize, he was already playing through various different scenarios for new rooms. Something to add more gore and more violence moving forward. Something to get the show feeling fresh again. After all, if it carried on like this, they would certainly start to lose viewing figures. Less viewing figures, less money. Less money, less potential to bribe governments into letting them carry on their games. Without the governments onside, no way would the games be able to continue. Worse than that, everyone involved would most likely find themselves facing an indefinite prison sentence… Shane wished he could give a surprise twist and just drop the contents of both hanging cages. Give the audience their gore fix by killing Victoria's parents *and* husband. Don't give her a prize. She did, after all, cheat in the last room. He looked towards the producer's booth beyond the studio audience and wondered whether they'd be up for that. Make Victoria choose and - then - make her watch everyone she loved die. With the bodies still warm, Shane could then explain to her and the audience why they had taken that course of action. He smiled at the thought. Would make for a great twist. If only he had control of the cage release. He could have just done it and then explained himself to the producers afterwards. Telling them his plan now though - yeah, not feasible… Can't explain his thoughts on air. It would look unprofessional. It would look even worse if the producers didn't go for it too because - obviously - the audience would be well up for it if they learned of it. You can't get the audience excited just to pull the rug from under their feet afterwards… You don't win fans that way.

Still, it's a plan that could possibly be implemented in the future. Hell, they could even have it changed so that - if someone cheated, like Vicki - they could be killed once they were out. Let them think they'd won and then - bam - invite an audience member down to drive a knife through their heart. Another plan to discuss ahead of the next season.

Stop thinking of the next season. Get this one done.

'I'm afraid I'm going to have to push you for an answer,' Shane said.

'I can't…' She asked, 'What is wrong with you fucks? Why are you doing this?'

'Tick tock… Remember, if you can't choose… We will simply take both prizes away from you…'

Vicki looked back up to her parents and husband. They were all looking right back down at her - fear evident in their eyes. Her father hugged her mother closer.

'Drop me,' Martin said gallantly. 'It's okay,' he said.

Vicki screamed.

'Who's it going to be?' Shane pushed her again as the audience continued shouting out who they felt should be chosen. But was that chosen to live or die? 'If you can't say it out loud - feel free to point up and we will take that as your answer.'

Vicki closed her eyes and screaming again. Her throat sore from all the screaming. She raised a finger and pointed. Her hand shaking.

'A good choice!' Shane yelled as the audience burst into applause. 'Release the other cage!' Shane shouted excitedly as the audience jumped to their feet to get a better look at when the contents of said cage were impaled onto the spike. Vicki covered her face with her hands and openly wept through her screams as the unchosen cage floor fell open and the contents within dropped. Even over the applause, the cheering, the shouting, her own screaming... She heard spikes split flesh and splinter bones.

The choice had been made. She screamed again - her face still covered.

'Well Victoria goes home with a prize she truly loves but was it the right choice?' Shane shrugged. 'For her it was.' He paused a moment before winking to the crowd. 'We hope you've enjoyed the show and we'll catch you next time... Remember - keep an eye on the site to see the next contestants we have lined up! Get your bets in and - who knows - maybe you can walk away a winner too!' Another pause. 'Until next time!'

The audience cheered as a curtain came down - separating crowd from stage. Game Over.

BONUS SHORT STORIES

In The Hand Of God

'I want to die.' His voice was drained of any and all emotion, with the will to live all but gone. This wasn't a new feeling. He had hit rock bottom some time ago when he lost the final thing that was important to him: his wife.

His name was Mark Joshua. Forty-five years old, dark hair, eyes as black as a bottomless pit. Soulless. He was married. He was a father of one child, a young boy of eight years. Mason. He was... *Was*. His wife had walked out, unable to cope with her own grief after the accident. Today he isn't a husband. Her grief and his anger being too much to bear. Now he was divorced. She had taken nothing away from him, even went back to her maiden name and yet - he felt as though he'd not only lost the love of his life but also his identity. And his boy? Today he isn't a father.

Today, he doesn't know what he is.

'Please...' Nervous. Afraid. The voice continued, 'I don't want to die.' A second man in a narrow bedroom halfway through being decorated. What had once been a child's room was in the process of being turned into... A spare room? An office? It had never been decided. She hadn't wanted to change it from what it had been and he... He hadn't known what the room should become. How do you make that kind of decision? 'Did you hear me? Please. I don't want to die.'

The second man's name was Ben Johnson. He was tied to a wooden chair, sitting opposite Mark who had a chair of his own. Between the two of them was a decorating table with marks of dripped paint and - in the centre - a black handgun.

'My boy didn't want to die,' Mark said. Still, no emotion. Monotone.

'It was an accident.'

'It was murder.'

The court case was imminent but it would be a day one of the two men wouldn't get to see. As the sun continued to rise on this new day, Mark couldn't say which of them wouldn't make it. He knew it wasn't up to him. It was up to God.

'It was an accident,' Ben repeated. His eyes had welled-up and the first tear rolled down his left cheek. He knew he wasn't being heard. Wasted breath.

'You *killed* my boy.'

A second tear quickly followed by a third. Still no emotion from Mark.

Mark viewed what had happened as murder whilst Ben knew it had been an accident. He wasn't a murderer. At least, not intentionally. Whatever their personal outlook on it though, it didn't change the fact that a little boy was dead.

Ben had been celebrating a promotion with a drinking session in the pub. What was supposed to be a celebratory drink turned into celebratory *drinks*. By the time he came to leave, he was wasted even though his drunken brain told him otherwise. He had climbed into his car and pulled out from the carpark, keen to get home to tell his wife the good news about the job. He hadn't made it five minutes down the road when it had happened…

'You took everything from me,' Mark said.

'I'm sorry.'

'Didn't even have the guts to face the consequences like a man. Tried to run. Coward.'

More tears.

'I'm sorry. Please. I'm so, so sorry... It was an accident. I was drunk, yes, but I never intended to hit your boy. I never meant to hurt...'

'Shut up!' *Anger.* Emotion at last. 'You had a choice. You chose to get in the car. You chose to drive home...' Mark shook his head. 'You *chose* to get drunk in the middle of the fucking day.' Mark's voice raised again, 'You killed my boy and you took everything from me! You destroyed my life! My job... My wife... I lost everything because of you!'

'I didn't mean...'

Mark interrupted him, 'I want to die. The problem is... I also want to kill you.'

'I have a family...'

'I *had* a family.'

'I'm sorry...'

'Fixes nothing.'

'If I could turn back the clock...'

Mark interrupted him again, 'The thing is, I'm not a murderer and suicide is frowned upon. Obviously there's a special place in Hell for you, you killed a person, but... Apparently you don't go to Paradise if you take your own life. That's right, isn't it? That's what you're told in church...'

Ben shook his head. 'I don't go to church...'

Mark stopped a moment. He looked at the scared man opposite. He doesn't go to church? Hardly surprising. This murderer. This monster.

'I've given this some thought though. Between my wife leaving me and snatching you from your home... I've given this *a lot* of thought. If I pick the gun up and shoot you dead - that's murder. If I pick the gun up and put it to my own head… Spray my brains on the wall… That's suicide. But… Leave the gun there, in the middle of the table, all I have to do is spin it. When the barrel stops spinning… Whoever it is aimed at… That's the person God has chosen to let die. Barrel points to you and He is allowing me vengeance. He is permitting me to send you straight to Hell. The gun points to me? God agrees that my time has come. He is giving me permission to take my own life but still granting me the right to sit by his side in Paradise…'

Ben didn't say anything. What could he say that wouldn't lead to more hostility? If there was a way out of this mess it would start with him keeping his calm and not angering the broken man further. But then - was there a way out?

After more thought, Ben said, 'I see your son every day. The look on his face just before the car… And I see his face when he is… Hit… I go to bed, I see it. I open my eyes in the morning and I see him… He is everywhere. The face of children I see in the streets… They're all the same. They're the face of your boy and…'

'You see my boy?' Mark asked.

'Yes. Everywhere I…'

'I don't see him.'

Silence.

Mark continued, 'Let's see what God thinks we should do.' Mark leaned forward to the gun and, with a strong hand, spun it in its place. Both men watched anxiously as the gun spun on the spot.

'Please. I have my own family. We don't need to do this. I'll be paying for what I did… I'll be pleading guilty… I'm not trying to hide anymore. I'm going to put my hand up…'

'Big of you.'

The spinning gun slowed to a rest. The barrel pointed between them.

'God clearly doesn't want either of us to die today,' Ben said, seizing his opportunity to try and talk his way out of this from another angle.

'He's undecided. Needs more time.' Mark leaned forward again and spun the gun for a second time.

'I'd give anything to turn the clock back and not get in the car. Anything to not drink… But I can't. It happened and I'm sorry. More sorry than you could ever imagine. I lie awake at night thinking of it - what I've done. I can't put it from my mind, along with the images of your little boy lying there… It's all I see… Day in and day out…'

The gun slows.

Panicking, Ben continues, 'It fucking haunts me and makes me sick. I can't eat, I can't sleep… Can't even look at my own children because I see your lad… And…' He stopped talking. The gun had settled. The barrel was pointing at him.

Mark shrugged. 'It appears God wants you dead.'

Ben shook his head. 'This isn't God's will. This isn't what he wants. This is chance. A sick game of chance…'

Mark leaned forward and picked the gun up.

'… Please don't do this.'

Mark pointed the gun at Ben's head. For a minute, he held it there with a shaking hand and his finger pressed against the trigger.

'Please…' Ben wept.

'You're right. This was a game of chance. I know that - not because you said so - but because I know, actually, God is dead. If he wasn't then my boy would be okay. My marriage would be fine. I'd be happy. But… Doing this has made me realise there is no point in killing you…' Ben didn't relax at the revelation. He couldn't. Not all the time the gun was aimed at his head. 'There's no point in killing you because there is no God which means no after life. I don't want to take away your guilt with a bullet. I want you to live a long, ugly life. I want you to see my boy every day of your miserable fucking life. I want it to continue eating you from the inside. I want your guilt to make you feel ill as you rot in a small prison cell… I want you to never forget what you did to my family. My world. And I want you to keep re-living this moment too…' Mark turned the gun to his own temple and pressed it hard against his sweating skin.

'Wait!' Ben shouted to no avail.

With no hesitation, Mark squeezed the trigger and took away his grief and pain. The gunshot momentarily drowned out Ben's desperate scream as a splatter of blood and brain decorated the untouched side of the child's bedroom.

Alone, ears ringing, a guilty man continued to weep.

The Body Out Back

1.

The peaceful dreams - reruns of happier days once lived - were shattered by the high-pitched shriek of the alarm resting on the bedside cabinet. Startled, Alex Davies sat bolt upright in his bed and hit the snooze button with his left hand. He winced in pain at a heavy swirling in the pit of his aching stomach that had been brought about by a sudden feeling of dread that washed over him. Unless the ache was from the previous night, lingering from his heavy night on the alcohol despite the doctor's advice? He slumped back down on the soft mattress, immediately falling back into the indentation his body had already made on it. Tired, and in pain, he sighed heavily. He had a pounding headache to go along with the burning sensation in his gut and there was no mistaking this for a feeling of dread. This was definitely down to the booze and he knew he only had himself to blame.

Just a couple more minutes, he thought to himself as he closed his eyes once more. *A couple more minutes and then I'll get up,* despite the temptation to reach for his charging mobile phone and call into work. It had been at least a month since the last sick day. Surely they wouldn't begrudge him another? It wasn't as though he did it every week.

2.

Alex's hand knocked the empty bottle of vodka onto the carpeted floor as it swung from the bed towards the alarm's ever-enticing snooze button. He lifted his weary head from the pillow and leaned over the edge of the bed to see what he had hit in his tired state.

A whole damn bottle?

He killed the alarm and sat up in bed.

Clearly he had been on a mission last night, not that he could remember much of it. There was the start of the evening, if he thought really hard and then - large black spots of nothing. It didn't bother him, not any more. He was used to missing time and, on the rare occasions someone had been there to fill him in with what had happened, he was grateful to lose the large chunks of his life to the ever-consuming black. It was easier to get on with your life when you weren't concerned with retracing your steps armed with a pitiful look and a half-arsed attempt at an apology for whatever misdemeanour you'd committed. With black spots, all he had to worry about when he woke up was whether he'd soiled himself and - even if he had - that was a quick fix with a warm shower and clothes in the washer.

Trying to ignore the banging in his head, Alex swung his feet to the floor and slipped his feet into the waiting slippers. No need for a dressing gown given the fact he was still dressed in the clothes he'd worn the night before; shirt and jeans - ruffled, creased and not suitable for a second day's outing.

Still giddy from the effects of the alcohol in his system, he staggered through to the en-suite bathroom. He squinted as the sudden illumination from above caused his head to pound further and - as quickly as he had turned the light on, he turned it back off. There was enough light spilling in from the master bedroom - curtains open - that he didn't need further lighting and, given the glimpse he'd caught of himself in the mirror's unkind reflection, it was better this way. He knew he was slowly drinking himself to death and didn't need to see the results of his actions. It wasn't as though such images would deter him from his desire to die anyway, they'd only serve to make him feel more guilty for those who had to bear witness to what he was doing. The people he was supposed to love. Those who begged him to seek help. Those who he continually pushed away and angered.

Alex grabbed his toothbrush from the silver holder by the sink with one hand and the toothpaste from another. That was the thing with alcohol, after the initial glasses, which were never pleasant, it always tasted so nice yet - the following day - the residues lingering in his mouth were both acidic and foul; almost enough to put a man off from wanting another drink. *Almost.*

3

'I'm really sorry,' Alex said to his line manager on the other end of the phone. 'I think it must have been something I ate,' he lied.

'Okay well thank you for letting me know.'

His manager, Sean, wasn't a stupid man and nor was he born yesterday. He knew it was less to do with something Alex had eaten and more to do with what he had drunk. Everyone in the office knew he had a problem.

'Can you call me at the end of the day and let me know if you think you'll be back tomorrow? That way I have a chance to organise some cover…' Sean continued.

'I'm sure I will be fine tomorrow but - yes, not a problem,' Alex said, fully aware that his hangovers tended to only last for one day, unlike his alcohol induced stomach cramps which had a tendency to last days, if not weeks. 'Again, I'm really sorry to let you down like this,' he said, trying his best to sound sincere.

'Okay. Hope you feel better soon.'

The line cut off as Sean put the phone down. He had said all he had to say for now, but Alex's absences would definitely play a part in the next review meeting. Oblivious to his manager's frustration, Alex tossed his phone down next to where he was sitting on the bed. Usually he would slip it in his pocket on the off chance someone would call or text but - the way he was feeling - he didn't need to speak to anyone else today. He was done.

Standing up, he caught his reflection in the full-length mirror in the opposite corner of the room. His brown hair was ruffled, stuck up in places, and his clothes were creased and dirty. He shrugged. *What does it matter? Not like you're going out.* His day was now to be nothing more than vegging in front of crap daytime television and perhaps a little hair of the dog to take the edge off the unpleasant hangover currently clouding him.

Knowing his appearance wasn't going to get any better, he turned from the room and headed down the stairs.

4.

Bills, bills, junk mail, more bills. Alex sighed. Sometimes he wondered why he even bothered collecting the mail up from the doormat. It was always the same old thing and never anything of interest. Bills, junk-mail in the form of leaflets from local delivery stores and random estate agents hoping he was looking to sell up, the local village news leaflet full of nothing remotely interesting to him and not a lot else.

He walked through to the kitchen with the post in hand, still flicking through what had come for him. Nothing of interest, or rather nothing that looked as though it needed immediate response so… He stopped in his tracks, his eyes stuck to the last envelope in the pile. It was a small DL envelope with a window. Unlike most letters that came like this, his name and address wasn't on display through the clear window of the envelope. Instead, only his name was handwritten across the envelope itself and, even then, his first name only. He frowned. Whatever it was, it had clearly been hand-delivered as opposed to posted along with the rest of the mail.

Alex tossed all of the mail on the side. He collected the kettle and took it across to the sink where he filled it half-full of water. Placing the kettle back on its cradle, he clicked the *on* button to get the water boiling before turning his attention back to the pile of post: The hand-delivered letter in particular. Without giving much thought as to whether he recognised the writing or not, he ripped into the envelope and pulled the folded sheet of paper from within. Ink could be seen through the folded page showing that there wasn't much of a letter to be read. One line, maybe two. Still confused as to what it could be, he unfolded the paper and read:

Do not disregard. Out of the back door, you will find a dead body.

'What the fuck?'

The words were handwritten in blue ink, sprawled across the lined-page with no attempt to even get it between the provided lines. Even though there wasn't much to read, and the chance of making a mistake with the meaning was slim, Alex scanned his across eyes the text for a second time and then a third. *Someone's having a laugh with you,* he thought to himself. He scrunched the paper into a tight little ball and tossed it towards the corner of the kitchen where the bin was overflowing. It landed on the floor next to a couple more empty bottles of alcohol which were awaiting a trip to the bottle bank.

The kettle clicked as it finished boiling with steam billowing from the nozzle.

Fuck 'em. Idiots.

5.

Alex was sitting at the kitchen table with his hands wrapped around the energy-giving mug of black coffee he'd prepared for himself. Normally he hated coffee but when you were this hungover, he'd found it to be the best medicine. Start with a mug of black coffee, maybe have a second. And then, after every last drop had been consumed, prepare yourself a full english breakfast lathered in heavy grease that was perfect for lining the fragile stomach - not that his mind was on the coffee. His mind was on the scrunched up note lying next to the bin.

Even if someone had been playing silly buggers with him, why would they bother? What could they possibly get out of it? They couldn't see his reaction when he opened the letter. They couldn't see his reaction as he approached the back door and neither could they see the look on his face when he opened it too, unless they were sitting out there waiting for him that is. But, even so, who would bother to do that?

He lifted the mug with both hands and took another sip.

It's just someone's idea of a sick joke, he thought. *Nothing more and nothing less and this... This reaction... This is exactly what they would have been hoping for. They would want you sitting here, curious to know whether there really was a dead body beyond the back door. Of course there isn't. That kind of thing doesn't happen around here.*

It was a good neighbourhood. The only time a corpse had been found around these parts was when one of Alex's elderly neighbours had passed away during the night. Their child had come visiting the next day and, unable to get them to open the door, had let themselves in with the spare key only to find their parent lying in their bed in an eternal slumber. A good way to go. With the exception of that morning, this neighbourhood was quiet. There had been little in the way of burglaries, if any. No cases reported of any domestic disturbances - which always made Alex chuckle given the arguments he used to have with his wife before she finally packed her bags and left - and there had certainly never been any cases of dead bodies lying just outside of the residents' homes. The letter was a sick prank designed to unnerve whoever received it and that was it.

Alex got up and fetched the scrunched up piece of paper. Returning to his chair, he smoothed it back out again so that he could read it for a fourth time. There was definitely nothing he had missed and this time - on closer inspection - he took a moment to examine the writing. He didn't recognise it.

He put the paper down on the table in front of him.

Alex chuckled to himself.

They'd have had better luck dropping it through the letterbox of someone at the nearby council estate. Dead bodies just aren't found here unless it's in circumstances like that old man... Or when I finally drink myself to death... Unless, of course, that cunt of a wife forces me to sell up as part of the divorce settlement.

With hot coffee in hand, he stood up and walked from the room. He was a drunk, yes. But he wasn't gullible.

6.

The plus side to receiving such a letter was that it had taken Alex's mind from the unpleasantness of the stomach cramps and pounding headache. Instead his thoughts were stuck on who would send such a pointless letter. To go to the effort of writing it, not that much writing was required, to finding out his name, to sticking it in the envelope and hand-delivering it. The whole thing was just damned stupid.

Unless, his mind teased him, *there is actually something outside the door.*

He stopped midway through to the living room where he had planned to spend the rest of his "sick day".

'All right then,' he said to himself, 'if only to shut you the fuck up.'

He turned back towards the kitchen and approached the rear door. With a confident hand he reached for the handle and gave it a twist before pulling the door open. No body slumped in.

'See? You're a fucking idiot and now you look like one too.'

He stepped out onto the patio area beyond the door and raised his hand in a wave-gesture towards the line of trees at the rear of his garden.

'Well done, you got me.'

First came a bang and then - a split second later - the pain. Alex dropped his coffee mug to the ground as his right hand reached to his chest. He collapsed to his knees and looked down to where his hand pressed against his burning chest. Red. So much red. He tried to speak but no words came out. Instead, he looked back towards the line of trees. A masked figure had stepped from beyond a thicket with a rifle in hand. They raised it to their eye-line and, without a word, pulled the trigger.

Alex's body slumped to the hard, cold ground with a hole in the chest and one in the centre of his forehead. Behind him, the kitchen door blew shut in a gentle gust of wind as the note drifted from table to floor on the very same gust. It landed in perfect alignment with the back door.

Do not disregard. Out of the back door, you will find a dead body.

The End.

<u>Insomnia</u>

<u>12:01am</u>

Oh good. Looks like I am set for another sleepless night tossing and turning, trying to get comfortable. What's that? The third night in a row where I get to watch the hours tick on by minute by minute, second by second? Yet, when I come to bed, I am shattered - barely able to keep my eyes open as I sit on the living room couch watching mind-numbing television shows which are meant to pass off as entertainment.

She is fast asleep. Of course she is. Taking up most of my side of the bed - spread-eagled there with her mouth agape and a little trail of saliva dribbling down to the damp pillow. She doesn't snore loudly but in my current frustrated state, it's enough to bother me. I can almost hear the taunting in the snores, *Oh, having trouble sleeping? Look at me. Look how peaceful I am.* There's a strong temptation to nudge her hard enough to wake her but I resist. After all, she has to get up for work in the morning. Perks of working from home, I can nap during the day if need be although - if I do - that will only cause sleeping issues for the following night.

I sigh and try to shift onto my side but, as if the wife isn't causing enough discomfort with the way she is crowding me, I have the damned cat by my feet too. Even she is snoring. She has been sleeping on the bed for most of the day, stretched out without a care in the world other than when we're going to next feed her. Well, she can get fucked.

I kick out with my feet and the cat flies from the bed. She does a strange twisting manoeuvre with her body, mid-air, before she lands on her feet with the gentle grace of a ballerina. Even having just been woken up she can still land on her feet. That's impressive. Despite the sudden kicking out, I don't want to actually hurt her. I just want some damned space to call my own.

The cat saunters out onto the landing and starts to eat her dried biscuits as though it had been her idea to get up, and not the fact I had booted her off. I roll onto my side and - for what feels like the first time in forever - move my feet. It feels blissful to not have a dead weight down there but I know it's a short-lived bliss because the cat will come back. She always does.

12:34am

She put the heating on before she came to bed. She usually does, nothing new there despite me telling her that - once she is in bed, under the duvet, she'd soon warm up. But - what do I know? I'm just the mug who gets to lie here sweating like a pig because it's too hot, and that's even with the window open in the desperate hope a cool breeze comes through.

I glance towards the fan in the corner of the room. Covered in dust, it hasn't been used since last summer when temperatures rocketed but there is a definite temptation to fire it up now. Looking at her, she's dead to the world. The sudden loud buzzing of a high-powered fan spinning won't stir her. But, if it does, she'll only complain that she is cold and ask me to turn it back off. Not just that, she'll moan that I woke her in the first place.

I roll onto my other side and try closing my eyes again in the hope sleep takes a hold of me.

01:20am

I have got to post various letters. Some are important, others not so much. I can probably post them the following day and just do nothing tomorrow. *Tomorrow?* It is "tomorrow". Sack the day off and crash in front of the television with my feet up. Maybe even walk to the nearby shop and treat myself to a bottle of red because - why not? Let's be honest, I might as well. I'm going to fucking useless at doing anything else. Hell, it's my turn to cook dinner tomorrow evening. Might just surprise the wife with a take-away…

I roll onto my back.

The moonlight is spilling in through a tiny crack in the curtain causing shadows on the ceiling that appear to change before my eyes to various different shapes and… monsters. I see monsters in the shadows.

Come on, stop thinking about crap like that. I don't need to be thinking about monsters, I don't need to be thinking about shapes and I sure as fuck don't need to be thinking about work - what I've done and what I need to do. Although, maybe I'm better off giving up on sleep and just getting up now. Carry on with my workload. No. That's stupid. I need to try and sleep. Even a few hours is better than none. Come on brain, turn off. Turn off brain, turn off.

<u>01:34am</u>

I thrash with my legs and kick the cat off again. Why does she always insist on sleeping on my side of the bed? My wife is dead to the world. She hasn't moved from being on her back for what seems like an age now. She has one hand by her side and one by her head. It doesn't look to be the most comfortable position but - like I said - she hasn't moved. So - with her so lifeless - why doesn't the cat go on that side? Instead, she jumps up on me and risks being booted off again.

Take the fucking hint, cat.

I close my eyes and raise my legs a little at the knees just in case she is stupid enough to try and jump straight back up here. To think, we've spent hundreds on cat beds and fancy posts with more sleeping areas built in. She'd rather be up here though, or in one of the cardboard boxes the cat beds came in. We should have binned the beds and kept those instead. At least then I might have got a comfortable night's sleep.

<u>02:07am</u>

It's not the cat that stops me from sleeping. It's the fucking heat. It's January. Why is it so stuffy in here tonight? Ah yes. Because *she* put the fucking heating on.

I push the duvet off and, for a split second, I feel some relief. The cool air instantly chills my overheated body which brings another problem. I start to itch as my skin crawls with the feeling of hundreds of little bugs running over me. Their tiny little legs tickling all over. I scratch the parts that I can reach. The ones that I can't just irritate and frustrate me further and then… Now I'm cold again as the breeze from the window reminds me that - yes - it *is* January.

I pull the duvet back over me and shiver for a split second before the warmth takes a hold of me once more.

Too much warmth.

'Fuck sake,' I mutter.

Why can't it be morning already? *It is.*

02:14am

I flick my right foot, tossing the duvet off it.

She chose this duvet. Must have been the thickest in the damned shop. There's no need for duvets like this in this country where, despite the rain, the weather tends to be fairly mild. I mean, I could understand if we lived in the Arctic or something but… Not here. No need. It's cold but it's not as though it is a blizzard out there.

Having my foot out of the duvet helps. Just one foot. It helps to regulate my body temperature although I can't stay here for long because…

… I flinch as the cat claws my foot.

'Fucking cat,' I hiss. 'Fuck off!'

'Wha….' my wife mutters as I pull her from her sleep.

Hiss!

I pause a moment as I realise the hiss hadn't come from down by my foot where I thought the cat was sitting, waiting to pounce again. Normally it's not just a case of one swipe and then a hasty retreat to the doorway. Usually she swipes at me continually until… I flinch and pull my foot back as I feel another swipe from sharp claws.

'Fucking cat!'

'What's she doing?' my wife asks.

The cat hisses from the doorway again.

'Sorry. I didn't mean to wake you,' I say before straining my eye-sight back to the hallway to see the cat. What the hell is she doing? Running over, swiping and then running back again? Little bitch. I reach for my phone, charging on the bedside unit, and power up its light. I shine the light towards the doorway half-expecting to see the bastard thing staring me out. She's sitting there as expected but she's not looking at me. She's staring at the floor by the side of my bed. With the light, I follow her harsh gaze and scream.

A pale-faced black haired-girl, with her bones twisted and contorted, stares at me from the floor with her eyes misted in death's shroud. Before I can do anything, she lunges at her - fingers outstretched with nails yellow and sharpened.

My wife screams too and - then - there is silence in the house.

Cold Hands

Marie worked hard for a living. The manager of a busy store, she left the house at around six in the morning and didn't come home until gone seven, after forty minutes or thereabouts of sitting in stationery traffic. The store opened at nine o'clock Monday to Saturday and an hour later on Sunday so she didn't *have* to leave the house that early. It was a choice. If she left later, she'd argue, she would get stuck in traffic and getting in early - when the store was still shut - had another benefit: It gave her the time to get paperwork done without frustrating interruptions. There was also the benefit of an uninterrupted cup of tea too.

The hours were long and mostly spent on her feet. Unlike other store managers within the retail environment, she didn't hide out back in the office surfing on her mobile phone's Internet whilst pretending to do *important stuff*. Instead she kept herself busy on the shop-floor, filling shelves, putting promotions on, working the tills and helping her staff in dealing with the many customers that came in - including those who had a shitty habit of trying to help themselves to the stock without paying. She was warned of those pricks from the previous manager who she had taken the job from when the last manager retired. Marie was used to people attempting to shoplift but even she wasn't prepared for the amount of idiots who would try their luck in this particular branch. But then, the store was in Portsmouth. What did she expect from England's arsehole?

After a long day she would get home, have some dinner and then - despite her best efforts - fall asleep on the sofa with the dog snoring on her lap and some crap on the television. When she would suddenly jolt awake, no doubt thanks to a snore of her own catching her by surprise, she'd realise it was pointless in trying to stay away when she was so clearly done in. It would be a far better idea to go to bed, get a semi-reasonable night and hopefully feel more refreshed in the morning.

'You're going to bed? Really? It's half-nine!' Matt would say.

'I'm sorry. I'm really tired.'

'Well, I'm not ready to come to bed yet so… I'll be up in a bit.'

That never stopped Marie from going on up. Matt would sit downstairs, on the sofa, with his feet up on the coffee-table - his eyes fixed to whatever was flickering on the television screen. The dog, having been moved from Marie's lap, would stagger over to Matt's where she would - once again - fall asleep. Clearly the dog had hard days too. She would spend them walking around the house, napping here and there and - of course - eating whatever crumbs she found lying on the floor. With the dog though, neither Matt nor Marie would mind when she fell asleep on them. It was better than having to run around the house making sure she wasn't eating something she shouldn't or, worse, shitting in some dark corner - maybe even tormenting the cat. A sleeping dog is definitely better.

*

The worst thing about going to bed early was not that Marie knew she would be woken again when her husband finally came up. It was the fact she'd be woken with his cold body - his hands in particularly - pressed against her own, warm body. It didn't matter how many times she asked him not to do it when he came up, he never listened. Even on nights when he shouldn't be as cold, he'd still press up against her and he would still be like ice.

'How are you so cold?' she would ask.

He would simply laugh and shush her quiet before saying, 'I'm not really here… You're dreaming it. Ssh…'

'You're an idiot.'

He would never reply, he'd would just snuggle in closer - his cold hands gripping her body, taking her breath away. Sometimes she wondered if he had gone and stood out in the garden just to get a chill to his skin before coming to bed. A cruel punishment for Marie daring to go to bed early. When she once asked him if this was the case he denied it but - to further make her question whether she was right - he would do so with *that* twinkle in his eye. A twinkle similar to that of a little school boy who was up to no good.

Usually when she felt his icy-touch, she would try and squirm from his grip - desperate to keep some of her warmth. She would beg him to let go, not that the devil ever would. He'd just snuggle in closer with *that* little laugh from the back of his throat. Tired, she would usually stop fighting him and reluctantly let him steal her body heat. Tonight though, when the bed-springs creaked as he climbed into bed and his cold hands touched upon her skin, she didn't pull away. Instead she pushed back in to him. She welcomed his freezing embrace and told him that she loved him. Usually he would reply. A line similar to, *I love you more.* But not tonight and not any other night moving forward. She knew that, if she were to turn around in his grip, he wouldn't be there.

Matt had passed away last week from a heart attack. His heart had been bad for a while with irregular beats that struggled to get the blood around his body. Last week, after his first run in some time, it simply gave up and he dropped dead leaving Marie a widow…

Leaving Marie wishing she could feel the cold touch of his hands.

Cold hands, warm heart.

Outfits

There was no time for her to shower but that wasn't a problem this evening. The client liked a bit of *au-natural* fragrance in her pussy as, he said, it accentuated the bitter-sweet taste. She didn't see it herself but didn't give a fuck. He was paying so could have whatever he wanted - within reason - so long as he didn't expect to kiss her afterwards, not that any of them tended to get to do that. Only *he* - Dan - got to do that. Or rather, used to do that before the snivelling, wretched, poor excuse of a human left her. Now it was back to *no one could kiss her*. Tonight's client wasn't really interested in kissing though. According to him, when it had come into conversation once, kissing was for idiots in love. He wasn't in love with Sarah. He was in *lust* with her, just as most of the clients who booked her for however long their fetish dictated. The only kissing the client enjoyed tonight was Frenching her lubed-up pussy or being *forced* to clean out her puckered asshole.

The dirtier the better, as far as he was concerned.

Sarah undid the belt to her unflattering uniform bottoms and slid them off. She kicked them to the side of her bedroom - not the room she'd be entertaining in - before removing her black thong too. She kicked it off and picked it up from the floor. Without a second thought, she rubbed it against her pussy and held it up to her nostrils. The client was in luck today. After a hard day on the prison ward, where she worked various shifts, she'd worked up a good degree of damp down there for him to feast on - *if* he was deserving enough.

She tossed the sweat-soiled knickers onto the bed, ready to shove in the client's face later when he would be trussed up, and scooped her trousers up before throwing those into the laundry bin. Couple of days off from *that* job now and wouldn't be needing the uniform again until next week. Or rather, *that* uniform. Quickly, she unbuttoned her blouse and dropped that into the laundry bin too, along with her bra.

Naked, her trim body on full display.

Sarah admired herself in the full-length mirror hanging on the wall for a moment, turning to the side. Her dyed red hair still looked clean, even glistening under the glow of the bedroom light. Her body - tight with a greyscale tattoo of an "evil" unicorn on her thigh. Her breasts large with erect nipples thanks, unfortunately, to the lack of heat in the room and not at the prospect of the impending appointment. Her bush, neatly trimmed right back. She turned her back to the mirror and checked out her rear. A great, smack-able arse - perfect for smothering the clients with and forcing them to clean out with their unworthy tongues. *Now* she felt a twinge in her vagina. Hell, tonight she might even let the client watch as she gave herself a long overdue orgasm - maybe even squirt in his face if she used the wand. She smiled at her reflection at the thought of getting herself off. Usually the appointments were just for the clients and she ended up walking away frustrated due to the fact she didn't permit intercourse with them but sometimes, when the mood took, she allowed them to see her bring herself off as she fucked herself with her favourite vibrator. *Don't you wish this was your dick inside me?*

Little bit wet.

She walked across to the furthest wardrobe in the room. The closest was every day clothes, the second was for work.

Hanging on the rails, various latex outfits; body suits in differing colours, but mostly black, a couple of catsuits, some hoods, skirts, dresses - some short, barely covering her pert arse, and others longer - to her knees… On the floor, beneath where they hung, different boots: Thigh highs, knee-highs, heeled, flat… And then, next to those, a few shelves that barely fit in there. On these were the rest of the outfits, the little pieces that made up the bigger, more dominant, picture: Stockings, panties, gloves, elbow length gloves, chokers and a couple of cans of spray that was used, as and when necessary, to shine the garments up. Latex looks incredibly sexy, worn tight on a confident woman. When it is left to dull down in colour, it looks cheap. Sometimes, even, tacky.

Sarah pulled out a black hood and one of the black catsuits, opting for the one which had the zip from arse to crotch. Keeping it zipped up, she can tease him with the promise of what is beneath. Then, when the time comes, she can work the zip and expose herself to his eager mouth. She picked out a pair of black gloves and took the entire ensemble over to the bed where she laid it out. It was fair to say she loved the tightness of the latex as it clung to her body but, getting it on was a real pain - often requiring liberal amounts of lotion on her bare skin first.

The client was due in near on half an hour. So long as he wasn't early, she had time to get it all on.

Sexy to wear, pain to get into.

*

'Can we try something new today?' were not the words Sarah had expected to hear from the client as he removed his coat. She should have known something was up due to the fact he wheeled in a suitcase.

It was perfectly acceptable to discuss the appointment's requirements in the hallway area. The session, her rules, did not officially start until they were in the makeshift dungeon - a small room out back which she had equipped with a St. Andrews' Cross and a spanking bench, along with a cupboard of *equipment* she had accumulated over the years.

'What did you have in mind?' she asked. 'I'm prepared for the usual,' she continued - suddenly concerned that she'd not yet washed from work and now, of all days, he might not be in the mood for *extra taste*.

'Well, I have some outfits that I would like to wear. I mean, we'd still do the same as usual to start off with but I'll be wearing an outfit... Then I'd put the other outfits on for you, at a time when you deem necessary... We'd play a little longer, whatever you want, and then I'd change uniforms again. I have three in total.'

She raised an eyebrow, somewhat curious. She couldn't remember the last time she had felt this way about an appointment. Usually they booked in, saying what they wanted and everything went to plan. It had been a while since someone had taken her by surprise.

'What kind of uniforms?' she asked.

'That's a surprise. When the time comes to change, you need to put a collar on me and lead me to the bathroom... I'll change and then, when I come out, you lead me back to the play room.' He asked, nervously, 'Would that be okay?'

Sarah tried to regain some composure. She needed to be the one in control and yet, by coming in here and changing what he usually opted for, he had tried to steal some of that from her.

'Would that be okay, Mistress?' she snapped.

The punter swallowed hard and asked again, 'Would that be okay, Mistress?'

'I suppose it would be but don't do it again without prior notification,' she ordered him.

'Yes, Mistress.'

'And my tribute?'

He reached into his pocket and withdrew the cash he'd saved from his monthly wage. One hundred and fifty pounds for an hour, although - often - the appointments tended to go over just a little bit. With a shaking hand (the norm, due to the anticipation) he handed the money over to Sarah who immediately took it off him.

'May I use your bathroom, Mistress?'

'You may.'

Sarah led the man to the bathroom. As he followed, watching her perfect, latex-clad arse wiggle, he dragged the suitcase of uniforms.

'When you're done,' she said in a stern voice, 'report to *the* room…' She pointed him to the relevant door and continued down the hallway of her home - back towards the kitchen to stash the tribute he'd paid. He was a regular client and knew exactly where *the* room was.

'Yes, Mistress.'

He stepped into the bathroom and closed the door behind him.

The client was a regular and had been for a little of a year now. A successful man in his fifties, it was clear that he liked Sarah as more than just a dominatrix - not that he was allowed to get that close. During a quiet time together, a few weeks into seeing each other for her professional services, he even dared ask her out for a drink. She shot him down in flames by saying it was disrespectful for a little maggot like him to even think he had the slightest chance of dating someone such as herself. To save from feelings getting hurt, she kept in character as she did it and promised only to see him again, when he next emailed, if he didn't "dare" discuss the idea of dating again.

He agreed.

*

More for the rent, Sarah thought as she put the money in the top drawer of the kitchen worktop.

She paused a moment, listening for movement outside. Nothing. With some time to spare, she fetched herself a glass before filling it with water. It was her third glass since getting home a little over an hour ago. She downed it in one, despite not being thirsty, and set the glass back on the side. She'd be pissing for Britain and he'd be fucking loving it.

'I'm ready, Mistress,' a meek voice called through the house as it made its way from bathroom to playroom.

Curious to see what he was wearing, Sarah left the kitchen and walked towards the playroom. He had already gone in and closed the door behind him. With her gloved hand, she reached up and twisted the handle before pulling the door open. She stopped dead in her tracks. Before her, her client stood in nothing more than a skimpy red dress, complete with hold-up stockings.

'I've been a naughty girl,' he said in a put-on high-pitched voice.

Sarah was grateful she was wearing the latex black hood as it hid her expression well. With a surprisingly calm tone of voice she replied, 'Then go and bend over that bench!' she ordered *her*.

The client turned to the far corner of the room where there was a kneeling bench made from a metal, black framework with red, leather perches. One perch to kneel on and then another for the victim's chest. On all four feet of the bench's framework, there were restraints waiting to be used. As the client made *herself* as comfortable as possible, kneeling forward with arse raised in the air, Sarah chose herself a cane. With one in hand, she gave it a couple of test swings - using her full force. It cut through the air with a swish sound and caused the client to flinch, much to her delight.

She turned to him and noticed that, beneath his skirt, he was wearing black panties.

'Hitch your skirt up,' she ordered him.

The client did as instructed and then gripped the framework of the bench. Sarah raised the cane high in the air and paused. The anticipation of the hit was half of the fun. A look to her client's face and he'd closed his eyes in preparation for the short, sharp sting.

'How naughty have you been, you little maggot?'

'I've been very naughty, Mistress.'

'And are you sorry?'

Before he could answer, she brought the cane down on his rear, causing him to yelp in pain. When she lifted it back in the air, ready for another swing, a red-lined mark had already appeared.

'I said,' she continued, giving the client a moment to compose himself, 'are you sorry?'

Again, before he had the chance to say one way or the other, she brought the cane down. This time it hit - and marked - his skin a little lower down causing another welt to appear. He yelped for a second time. This time, when she raised the cane, she didn't ask the question a third time. She just brought the wooden bamboo down with another almighty wallop.

Whatever stress occurs during the day, this always helps alleviate it.

The client yelped.

'I'm sorry, Mistress!' the client screamed out. 'I'm sorry!'

'How sorry?'

She raised the cane again and struck for a fourth time. The client screamed out in pain as a fourth line appeared across his exposed arse cheeks. To people looking in, from the outside, it could have looked as though she were inflicting pain and - whilst she was - he didn't mind. All of her clients knew the safe word when they crossed into her world. If they wanted her to stop - all they had to do was say the word *red*. Sarah had been working as a professional dominatrix for over two years now and - during that time - only one person had said the safe word and that wasn't because she hurt had hurt them. The client had said it before the session had even properly started.

He had been lying on the floor, trussed up tight with clear film wrapped around every part of his body - including his hard dick. Beneath him was plastic sheeting to protect the floor and, over his head, was a special stool Sarah had purchased; a metal frame with a toilet seat on the top of it. It was here Sarah would have sat to relieve herself over the man's pathetic face. Not just a warm trickle of a golden shower but also… It was at this point the client spoke up with the safe word. When asked why, after he'd been released and Sarah had come back from the bathroom, he stated it was because he had suddenly realised it would be better left as a forbidden fantasy. Sarah did not judge the man for chickening out at the last minute, just as she didn't judge the men (and sometimes ladies) who came to her with strange fetishes. If anything, she respected these people for having the guts to stand up and share this part of their world with a complete stranger, albeit a stranger who guaranteed discretion on her website…

The other clients, the ones who saw their fantasies through to the end, didn't say the safe word because, as time went on, Sarah had come to learn to read the signals. For instance; another two, quick, successive blows from the cane on this client's tender looking arse and it was clear that he was getting to the point of having had enough.

Sarah stroked the back of his stocking-clad legs with the cane, teasing and yet, at the same time, somewhat threatening.

'And will you be naughty again?' she asked him.

There was a slight pause as the man composed himself, forcing his mind to forget the stinging pain he was in. 'No, Mistress.'

'Good. I believe you.'

She walked around to the front of him and made a show of leaning the cane on the wall. He knew he was safe now. At least, safe from anymore of that type of punishment. There'd be something else up her latex sleeve, not that he minded.

'You look like a pretty little girl,' Sarah said. 'I bet all of the boys love you...'

'They do, Mistress.'

'I bet that all try and *fuck* you.'

'They do, Mistress.'

She walked back around the spanking bench and ran her gloved-hand over his arse.

'I think I might like to fuck you,' she said before giving him a playful smack.

'I'd like that, Mistress.'

'I bet you would, you dirty little bitch.'

She walked to a double bed at the far side of the room. The bed was covered in a black heavy duty vinyl bed-sheet, already prepared for messy fun. She sat on the edge of it.

'I want you to dance for me,' she said.

The client, not daring to move for doing wrong, turned to her.

'Come and dance for me. Don't make me *think* I want to fuck you. Make me *want* to fuck you,' she told him.

The client got up from the bench and crossed the room to where Sarah was sitting, after pulling his skirt down. Sarah opened her legs as much as the tight catsuit permitted.

'I want a lap dance,' she told him.

The client hesitated a moment and then started to awkwardly sway from side to side, clearly not much of a dancer. Sarah laughed at him.

'Is that it?' she asked, still laughing. 'You're not making me feel like I want to fuck you,' she said.

The client stepped between her legs and started to sway his hips from side to side again, slower this time as he imagined some tune playing in his head. As he swayed, he started to run his hands over his body - his chest, imagining he was running them over a pair of perfect, pert breasts. He turned, putting his behind in her face, as he continued swaying before finally bending over. The short skirt hitched up enough for her to see his black thong beneath. He looked back at her and smacked his arse, trying not to wince as the flat of his palm caught one of the six welts.

Sarah watched unimpressed, although there was something about the fact he was wearing a dress that caused her to feel a little moist. His masculine hands running over the silk-like material of the outfit he'd chosen for himself. Even the way that it actually seemed to suit his average figure - somehow making it look as though he had a better shape than he actually had.

'I hope you fuck better than you dance!' Sarah mocked him. 'Get back over there on that bench,' she said.

'Yes, Mistress.'

Doing as ordered, he crossed the room and knelt down on the bench, once more exposing his rear to his Mistress.

As Sarah walked back to the cupboard filled with the various toys she had at hand, she teased him, 'I think the boys like to fuck you out of sympathy,' she said. 'They don't find you sexy,' she continued. 'They just want to know if you fuck as bad as you dance...'

'I know, Mistress.'

Opening the cupboard doors, her eyes went straight to the various strap-ons. There were three in total and, over the years, they'd all had their fair share of use;

mostly for men in high positions of power. She never questioned them why. She could guess why they liked a fucking.

She reached for the middle strap-on. A bumpy-textured glass dildo locked into a pink harness that secured around her back and tightened further on her thighs - really keeping "the dick" in place. Removing it from its shelf, she stepped into it and pulled it up before tightening the straps. Next, she took a hold of the bottle of lube, next to the remaining strap-ons, and squirted a liberal amount over the tip of her cock. Replacing the bottle, she used the other hand to smear the dolloped lubricant over the rest of the dildo until the whole thing was slippery. Ready for action, she grabbed a small popper from the same shelf and walked back round to the front of the client. His eyes fixed on the nine inches of glass that was about to be inserted into him.

'Tell me, you dirty fuck, do the boys ever fuck you with something this big?' she asked.

'No, Mistress.' He continued, 'That's a beautiful cock, Mistress.'

She removed the lid from the poppy and held the small jar under his nose.

'Sniff, bitch!' she ordered him.

The client didn't hesitate. She breathed in the toxic fumes of the popper, a little jar of various chemicals mixed together which had been developed to make a person's muscles relax completely. Before he'd even finished breathing in the fumes, he felt his face start to flush and his brain tingle. Sarah replaced the lid, set the bottle down and walked to his rear.

'I'm going to make you my bitch,' she warned him.

'Please, Mistress.'

She nudged the tip of her cock against his potentially virgin arsehole and slowly pressed forward. A slow push to ensure no discomfort was caused as she made her way past the sphincter muscles. The client gasped and she held herself in position - neither moving forward further or pulling back. A couple of seconds later and she pushed forward slightly again, all the time reading his body signals. If he tried to pull away, she would pause - leaving her dick perfectly still. The moment she was in and he pushed back, she knew she had the green light to fuck him how he wanted to be fucked.

'Dirty bitch,' Sarah said again as the client took the full amount of the glass dick. 'Dirty fucking bitch, you like that?'

'Yes, Mistress.'

'How much?'

'I love it, Mistress.'

'Tell me how you love my cock.'

'I love your cock, Mistress.'

'Then take it,' she told him as she started to fuck him.

At first she started fairly softly, gently even. Penetrating him with the care that a first time lover might demonstrate to someone they cared about. It didn't take long for that to change though as she started to increase her speed. A slow love-making gradually turned to a hard fucking. She was grunting with each strenuous push forward and he was grunting having his arse stretched open and taking the full length of the dick in.

Sarah suddenly stopped fucking him and smacked the client's arse with the palm of her hand when she realised he'd reached back and started stroking himself.

'Don't you dare fucking do that!' she warned him. 'Unless,' she continued, 'you'd like for me to stop and get the cane again?'

The client pulled his hand away and grabbed the leg of the bench again. Satisfied he had obeyed her, Sarah started to fuck him again only this time - she didn't go gentle. She thrust forward deep and hard and the client screamed out loud and continued to do so as she pounded him at the same speed.

'That's it, you dirty cunt. Take it all.'

She carried on fucking him, holding her hands on his hips to keep him in place as each thrust went as deep as his arse permitted and - then - with no warning, she pulled the dick out.

'Your outfit bores me,' she said.

She loosened the straps of the dildo's harness and the toy fell to the floor.

'Go and change!' she ordered him.

Tentatively, the client got up from the bench.

'Yes, Mistress, thank you, Mistress.'

Sarah went and sat on the edge of the bed as the client disappeared from the room, heading back to the bathroom for his second outfit.

Feeling a little turned on from fucking his arse like that, Sarah took the alone time to stroke her moist pussy through the latex. It hadn't been the first time she had seen a man dress as a woman although it was obvious, from this client, that it was *his* first time of doing it. Usually they came complete with wig and make-up. Some of them even surprised her by giving *her* tips on how to apply make-up with a skill set which outshone her knowledge. She thought that some of those men, when dolled up like that, looked hot and, on some occasions, she'd been tempted to reward them by letting them fuck her. *Tempted to.* No one got to actually fuck her other than Dan and now he was gone… She stopped stroking herself as her mood momentarily darkened at the thought of the weasley little prick.

Why let him get to you? He keeps walking out on YOU and yet you keep letting him back in your life like a fucking idiot.

The last time he had walked out had been the final straw. Now if he came back, even begging, she would tell him to fuck off. It was one thing for someone to keep coming and going, unsure of what they really wanted, but when she found out he was cruising the dating sites again…

Fuck him.

She forced the thoughts of Dan from her mind. Now was not the time to be thinking of the pathetic cunt. Now was the time to be professional and provide a service that the client sought, not to let thoughts of Dan force you to accidentally *murder* a client as you pictured dickhead Dan in their place.

Stop thinking about him. Think about the client… What's the next outfit going to be?

The question thankfully stuck in her mind. What *was* the next outfit going to be? If the first was a dress then what would follow? A nappy? He'd come in as a baby? It wouldn't be the first client to have wanted to be an adult baby - another service she was happy to provide; grown men in diapers looking to be pampered. Nothing ever sexual, she wouldn't permit that… She would literally just pamper them as though they were a real infant child.

He wouldn't.

She guessed that, if he had been going to wear a nappy, maybe he would've started off in that and then progress to the girl? It would have made sense. He could have retained the same "character" throughout the whole appointment.

Young baby, followed by dirty slut as the baby turns to woman, followed by…
What would come next? He'd dress as a grandmother? *That* was something Sarah
was yet to see. Her heart skipped a beat at the thought of it. Even she wasn't sure
she'd be able to keep a straight face for that…

*

'You took your time. Are you trying to annoy me?'

'No, Mistress.'

The client was standing in the playroom doorway. He was wearing an all-in-
one PVC outfit complete with a black hood mask, black PVC socks and PVC
gloves. Although it was currently open, across the mouth of the hood - there was a
zipper. Sarah didn't show it but, given where her mind had been going with what
he could have dressed in, she was a little disappointed. On the plus side, it made
the next part of the appointment easier for her as she could tie it in with his usual
"tastes".

'Don't just stand there like a fucking idiot, slave, get over here.'

The client walked over to where Sarah was sitting on the bed. He stood in
front of her. She ran her hand down the body of his PVC outfit and - without
warning - slapped his rather obvious erection through the material.

'What the fuck is that?'

'I'm sorry, Mistress.'

'You disgust me.'

She stood up.

'Wait there.'

She went back to the cupboard and pulled out a roll of film that came on a handy dispenser.

'Your Mistress has had a long and hard day,' she said as she crossed back to where he was standing, his erection still showing through his outfit, 'and is in need of a bath…'

'Yes, Mistress.'

Starting at his shoulders she started to mummify him with the film.

'You're a pathetic shit,' she said as she worked.

'Yes, Mistress…'

'… So you should feel honoured that I am going to let you do this.'

'Yes, I do, Mistress.'

'… So you had better not disappoint me,' she warned him.

'I won't, Mistress.'

'If you do, there will be consequences!'

'I understand, Mistress. Thank you.'

Sarah wrapped him right down to his ankles and then tossed the film-dispenser to one side. She stood there a moment and admired her handiwork. He wasn't going anywhere fast. Satisfied he was her prisoner, she pushed him back on the bed. He bounced on the soft mattress and then Sarah took him by the ankles and swivelled him round so that he was both entirely on the bed and as comfortable as could be.

She stood next to the bed and carefully undid the zip of her catsuit, exposing both pussy and arse to the coolness of the air. Without needing to even touch it, she could feel that her skin was damp from sweat.

'Mistress has had a very busy day,' she said.

She backed up so that she could sit back on the second highest section of the bench. Perched there, she opened her legs wide, exposing her cunt for the client to feast his eyes open. Looking him dead in the eyes, she started to suck on her gloved finger before running her hand down her body - over her firm breasts, down her stomach, all the way to her pussy.

'Mistress has been running around punishing worthless pieces of shit like you,' she said in a stern voice. 'Worked up quite a sweat and hasn't had a chance to wash yet...' The clients didn't know about her "real" job, working in the prison. She knew most wouldn't care but - for some - it would ruin the illusion of who she was. They didn't want to think of her in a normal, everyday setting. They wanted her to be this all-powerful woman who answered to no one.

Her finger glided over her glistening cunt and she sighed in pleasure. The client strained against the film but wasn't going anywhere until she said so. She had made sure of that.

'Please let me clean you, Mistress...' he begged.

Pathetic.

'Poke your tongue out,' she told him.

Without needing to be asked twice, he poked his tongue out of his mouth and held it there.

'Not bad,' she told him, 'considering the rest of you is useless.'

She got up and crossed the room back to the bed. She climbed on and positioned herself over the client's mouth, his tongue, just out of reach.

'Can you smell how dirty my cunt is from there?' she asked.

He put his tongue back in his mouth momentarily and breathed in deeply. A day's worth of sweat clinging to her lips like a cheap perfume, 'Yes, Mistress.'

Without needing to be asked, and not wanting to delay what was coming, he stuck his tongue back out.

Sarah lowered herself so that only the tip of his tongue could reach her scented labia. When the client cranked his neck forward to try and get a better reach, she teasingly pulled away.

'I want every part of that cunt spit-polished,' she told him before lowering herself towards the tip of his tongue once more.

He moaned softly as he licked as much as she permitted him to reach. Looking down, despite the PVC outfit and the film wrapped tightly around him - she could see the outline of his bulging dick. No doubt he was desperate to be inside her.

Too bad for him.

A few more licks of his warm, wet tongue against her labia and Sarah squatted above him slightly, again pulling herself away from his reach - much to his frustration. Beneath the film he was clearly trying to move his hands to his cock. Not going to happen. The wrap is too tight. She smiled to herself at the torment she was causing him.

'Open your mouth wide for your Mistress,' she said.

The client shuddered in anticipation of what was to come. He had been in this position many times before, but only with Sarah. A couple of seconds passed by and - then - the flow started. Slowly at first, a few trickles, until it turned to a warm, constant stream of pure golden nectar - splashing him across his covered face and going into his mouth where he willingly swallowed it down.

'Drink it up, slave!' she said. 'Don't you dare spill a fucking drop...'

The client didn't speak. Instead he lifted his head up off the bed to try and get closer to the steady flow, only putting his head back down on the mattress again when it was but a trickle and - then - nothing. He swallowed again and licked the piss from his lips.

'I need further cleaning,' Sarah said. This time she lowered herself right down onto his face as she started to smother him. Immediately she felt the client's tongue push inside her, taking advantage of how generous she was being with her body. She felt him snake it around inside her, leaving no part untouched as the client frantically tried to find the sweet-spot to ensure she'd want to stay.

Not quick enough.

Sarah raised herself slightly and repositioned herself. When she came back down - her full weight once more - it was obvious that she didn't require her sweet pussy to be cleaned anymore. She sighed in pleasure as she felt the client's tongue rim her arsehole before pushing in as deep as it could reach, tasting all that was to offer. Occasionally, she lifted herself slightly to allow him another gulp of air before coming back down - full weight again - on his face. He writhed around beneath her in ecstasy as his Mistress permitted him to keep tonguing her arsehole. Unseen by the client, she reached down and started circling her clitoris with two fingers closed together.

Why should the clients have all the fun? she thought to herself as she let the tickling sensation around her ring, and the sensitivity of her clitoris being rubbed start the slow process of building her towards an orgasm.

She lifted herself slightly.

He breathed.

She lowered herself.

He continued licking and tonguing.

'Considering how pathetic you are in everyday life,' she said - trying to hide the pleasure from her voice and retain the strict authority she wanted projected, 'you're doing a good job. If you carry on,' she continued, 'Mistress might just let you climax at the end.'

She lifted herself.

'Thank you, Mistress.'

She lowered herself.

Not all appointments ended with the client climaxing. Some went away feeling just as frustrated as she had made them during the appointment. Only the well-behaved clients were permitted the climax and - even then - it was by their own hand only as Sarah watched over them, giving them instructions as to what to do to themselves. They never seemed to last more than a couple of minutes before they shot their load into the rubber condoms provided (Mistress wouldn't tolerate sticky mess).

Squatting over his face, fingering her cunt as he continued alternating between rimming her and fucking her arse, Sarah reached up with her spare hand and squeezed her breast hard, pinching the nipple through the latex as best she could.

'Mistress is going to cum,' she said, without lifting.

Her words were all that were needed for the client to resort back to just tongue-fucking her arse as deep as he could get it. Not wanting to deny herself the pleasure, Sarah screamed and rode out the orgasm as it hit - causing her whole body to shudder and her pussy to spasm around her fingers. She felt her face flush beneath the latex hood as she raised herself from the clients face once more - allowing him to gulp in some more air.

'Thank you, Mistress,' he said.

'I've had better,' she told him, regaining control of the situation. 'You don't deserve the climax I offered earlier. I think I want to leave you feeling sexually frustrated.'

'Please, Mistress...'

'Beg!'

'Please, Mistress... I want to climax. Please let me. Talk me through it, Mistress. Please!'

'Ha! You're pathetic.'

She clambered off the bed and crossed the room back to the wardrobe. She reached in and pulled out a pair of scissors before walking back to where the client lay helpless. Slowly - carefully - she started to cut through the binding allowing him to be free.

'Your outfit bores me,' she said sternly. 'Go and change it.'

The client sat up and moved to the edge of the bed. He didn't move for a moment. He pulled the hood from his head. He didn't say anything but Sarah could tell from his face that something was on his mind.

'What's the matter? Are you scared Mistress won't approve of the next outfit?' She asked in such a way that she kept in character *but* gave him a get out of having to dress up if he had suddenly changed his mind.

He hesitated a moment and then shook his head.

'What's that supposed to mean?' Sarah asked sternly.

'No, Mistress.'

'No, Mistress? What are you talking about? Did I deprive you of too much oxygen when I sat on your face?' she continued.

'No, Mistress.' He explained, 'No, Mistress, I haven't changed my mind about the last outfit. It's just that it might take a little while to get ready and so... Would you be willing to accept further tribute for some more time?'

Sarah frowned. If he needed more time for the appointment, it should have been organised before the session started. After all, he didn't know whether she had another client due that she'd have to get ready for. On this occasion, he was lucky, she didn't have another session booked in.

The client spotted he'd annoyed her with his question.

'I'm sorry, Mistress, I didn't think.'

'Of course you didn't think. You're a pathetic piece of shit.'

'Yes, Mistress.'

'Well don't just stand there,' she said, 'hurry up and get the next outfit on. We can discuss further tribute if it is required at the end of the session.'

'Yes, Mistress. Thank you, Mistress.'

He hurried from the room. Hot from the latex, and hungry for dinner after a busy day at work, Sarah perched herself on the edge of the bed and waited for him to return. As she did so, she reached up and pulled the hood from her head. She tossed it to the corner of the room, knowing she'd be having to clean up later anyway, and ruffled out her hair.

Nice for the air to get to bare skin.

She glanced to the small clock on the floor, in the corner of the room beyond the wardrobe. A digital clock that was small enough for most people to not notice but easy enough for her to see the time - to ensure the appointments didn't run over too long. She didn't mind ten minutes here and there but, she had the draw the line somewhere.

They had so far been forty minutes. He had booked in for an hour. If he was quick getting changed, and she was quick with his *reward* then there was a good chance she would have him finished in his booked time. No need for further tribute.

If he's ready soon. How much longer is he going to be?

*

Fifteen minutes.

Sarah turned to the playroom door as it opened. Her heart skipped a beat as her client walked in, dressed in a clown's outfit:

She wished she had kept her latex hood on; help disguise the shocked look on her face.

Garish green trousers, a lime shirt that clashed with a purple velvet jacket which had a white plastic flower in the lapel. His face had been powdered white with red rings around his eyes and over his mouth - not applied with care or precision. On his hands were white cotton gloves and - uncharacteristically for a clown - his feet were bare. His hard-on - exposed.

Sarah tried to remain in character, 'You look as pathetic as I first believed you to be.'

'That's right.'

'I beg your pardon?'

Trying to keep the control she needed, she got up from the bed and grabbed the cane from where she'd left it earlier. She pointed the tip towards the ceiling in a threatening display; a promise to swing down if rules weren't followed.

'I'm dressed exactly how you see me on a day to day basis.'

'Mistress. You will address me as Mistress.'

'I'm a clown,' he continued, ignoring her rules, 'I'm a fucking joke to you...'

Sarah frowned and took a step back. She realised that this appointment wasn't going the way it was supposed to. She'd lost control, he'd lost respect. The business relationship had crumbled and - in those last few seconds - the session was over.

'Time's up,' Sarah said abruptly.

The client simply shook his head.

'No. It's not. Now it's time for a *different* kind of session.'

Before she had a chance to react, the clown lunged forward and - with a hand to her throat - shoved her back onto the bed. Immediately, she went to get up - only to be stopped when he climbed on top, his weight holding her in place. He took a hold of each of her wrists and pinned her hands up by her head.

'I *loved* you,' he said.

'No, you didn't.'

'I did. I asked you out and you slammed me down.'

'Our relationship was one of a professional standing.'

'No, no, no... That's not right... You *liked* me too...'

'Not as a partner!' She changed the subject, 'Please get off me.'

'I came back to see you, all this time, thinking you would change your mind...'

'It was a business meeting! That's all!'

'You took my money over and over again...'

'It's my job too... Get off! You're hurting me!'

'You took me for a mug. A *clown*...'

'I didn't. I treated you as a client!'

'I lost everything. I've sold things to keep seeing you. I've downgraded my life for you... All because you wouldn't give me the chance to treat you as a man should...'

'It's a business relationship. Nothing more and nothing less. I made it clear. I even said in the email, when you contacted me again... I told you then that it would never be anything more than...' She continued, 'I don't date clients!'

'That's *your* rule you put in place! You could have broken it.' He continued, 'All this money - seeing you - and I never got to have the appointment with you that I really wanted. I never got to stick it in you. Never got to fuck you...'

'I don't offer that kind of...'

'Well - today's different. The clown has the final laugh.'

He released her left wrist long enough to grab his still-hard member and guide it toward her cunt. She tried to push him off but, with only one wrist and his weight still pushing down on her, she was trapped. He thrust into her, deep and hard. She gasped out loud from both the shock and the pain.

'You're my fucking bitch now.'

With her free hand, she scratched his face.

'Fucking bitch!'

He grabbed her wrist and pinned it back again to the side of her head as he continued fucking her bareback.

'It would have been different,' he said as he penetrated her, 'I would have treated you like a gentleman… I would have… Treated you right…'

'Get the fuck off me!' she hissed - venom in both tone and eyes. She wriggled around underneath him, trying to free herself and shake him off. In her line of work, she was used to having to restrain big, burly men when they got out of hand but when they'd already seized control of the situation, it was ten times harder. Worse yet, she should have expected it - or at least been prepared for it. Working in the prison, she'd seen the ugly side of them.

Should have never accepted that appointment.

'Your cunt feels so fucking wet… Tell me you're not enjoying this…'

'Fuck you…'

Her pussy would have been wet from the saliva he'd licked into it. It had nothing to do with her state of arousal - or rather, lack of. The moment she saw him standing there, dressed as a clown, had dried her vagina up faster than a sponge.

'I could just fucking cum right here and now,' he sighed as he continued pounding her. 'But I won't…' He pulled out and his dick hit her thigh as she breathed a sigh of relief. 'Not yet anyway.' He got up and yanked her to her feet. On instinct, she hit him hard across the face in the hope it would shock him long enough for a getaway. Turned on, and running on adrenaline, he barely even flinched as he responded with a heavy slap of his own which knocked her to the floor dazed.

'Little cunt,' he spat.

Before she had a chance to come to her senses, he picked Sarah up and threw her down over the spanking bench. She went to say something, another request to let her go, but was hit for a second time - this time straight in the back of her head.

A short punch designed to stun. All Sarah's power had gone now as she started to weep - both pain and fear overriding her internal system - as the clown fastened her into the restraints.

With Sarah locked in place, already struggling as she begged for her release, the clown picked the cane up that she'd used on him. Without any words, he thwacked it hard against her latex-clad buttocks. She screamed in pain, and for a second time as he swung again with just as much force.

'Yeah, it hurts, doesn't it?'

He tossed the cane down to the floor and got down on his knees behind Sarah's rear - her crack still exposed thanks to the open zip.

'What I will say, though, is that your arse tastes fucking fantastic...'

He pushed his face between her buttocks and started rimming her once again, a selfish act for himself and nothing to do with how it might be pleasant for her. In the short-term, *all* for him. In the long-term, *preparing her*.

He pulled out briefly, 'I could just fucking lick this all night long,' he said. He buried his face into her arse again, poking his tongue back into her puckered hole, as she continued weeping despite her best efforts not to. She was a strong woman. She didn't cry. This wasn't her. But then...

... She was usually careful not to put herself in this position.

'Yummy!' he stood up and positioned the head of his thick dick against her tight hole. No pause. He pushed inside until he was balls deep, causing her to scream out loud.

'It's not that bad,' he teased her having been on the receiving end earlier. 'You can take it.' With no mercy he started to fuck her arse hard and deep with a little extra push each time his shaft was swallowed up to the balls in the hope he could get a little deeper.

Sarah was screaming as she coated his cock in both traces of faeces and blood, not that either bothered him as he was too caught up in the feeling of how tight she was.

The clown suddenly moaned out loud as an intense orgasm caused his legs to buckle and his body to lose all sense of rhythm as it shuddered through the after effects. His thick, creamy load shot deep into Sarah's anal passage with some immediately trickling out - a mix of brown, red and white - as he withdrew his spent cock.

'Fuck me,' he said breathlessly. 'Sorry… I have a feeling that was shit load. Only yourself to blame, though, with the way you wind me up.' He took a breath, 'Fuck that was good.'

Sarah didn't say anything. She just laid over the bench with tears - near enough under control - still lingering in her eyes.

Should have seen the signs. Should have seen the signs. Shouldn't have carried on seeing him after he'd admitted that he had feelings past client and professional. Stupid, stupid girl…

'My partner is due home,' she said, making no attempt to look at the clown.

The clown came round to the front of the bench and crouched down so that he was level with her face.

'How is Dan?' he asked.

Sarah looked at him - alarmed that he knew Dan's name.

'Come on, Sarah, don't be shy…'

And *her* name.

He continued, 'How is he?'

'Fuck you.'

'I know you two aren't a couple anymore. But I also know he is completely fine with what I am doing now.' He paused. 'Want to know how I know?'

Sarah didn't answer him.

'Because,' the clown smiled, 'he wanted to join in...'

Sarah frowned.

He knew?

'Plot twist!' the clown shouted. 'How exciting! Yep, your ex wants to make this a threesome! See, had we been a couple, I would have said no. I would have said, no - sorry... I don't permit that of my partners. I think it is disrespectful but - seeing as you're nothing to me... Just a fucking *whore*...' He shrugged. 'I don't see why we can't have a threesome, right?' He paused another moment. 'In fact, fuck it, why not?'

Leaving Sarah bound and vulnerable, the clown stood up and walked towards the playroom door. A quick glance behind to Sarah's exposed arse, along with a *mmmm-hmmmm* from his mouth, he suddenly stopped in his tracks. His eyes had fixed on the semen trickling from her ruined hole. He tutted and walked back across to her and - with his gloved hand - he mopped up the trickling gunk. With it coated on his glove, he leaned forward and forced it into Sarah's mouth, scraping the semen, shit and blood on her bottom teeth. Sarah gagged as the clown walked back towards the door.

It was mind games, that was all. Dan was a cunt, a deplorable piece of shit, but he wouldn't be a part of this. No way, Sarah kept telling herself over and over again.

Footsteps from the door behind. She strained to see who had come back in couldn't twist enough.

'Dan?' she called out.

No one answered. The footsteps came closer.

'Dan?' she called again. 'Undo these restraints,' she ordered him. 'Let me out!'

Sarah had always worn the pants in the relationship. Looking back, she couldn't even see why she had been going out with him for so long other than - potentially - a fear of being alone and a promise of being treated well. He wasn't even worth keeping around for the sex, though, with his small dick and inadequate moves. Regardless, if he was in the room, it would be easy to get him to free her from the bindings.

'HEY! BABY!'

Dan's severed head appeared in Sarah's vision - held there by the clown who was laughing hysterically - causing her to scream uncontrollably.

Mocking Dan's voice, heard only once when he went to take his head, he asked, 'So - baby - fancy a little head?' He laughed again and then, in his own voice, said, 'Well, we're all here... I think it's time we got this fucking party *started*!'

*

The clown was standing in front of Sarah who was still restrained to the bench. He had set the *Versa Fuk Machine* up behind her; a powerful motorised machine which thrust a metal pole back and forth, onto which a dildo was usually attached.

The person on the receiving end of the machine, fucked at whatever speed the machine's operator chose for them. The client had been on the receiving end of a high-speed fucking one particular day when Sarah had felt crueller than usual. Tonight, it was *her* turn to be on the receiving end.

'How's that?' the clown asked as he increased the machine's tempo.

Unlike when he had been anally fucked by the machine, this time there was no dildo on the end of it. Instead he had stabbed the metal arm through Dan's decapitated head, hard enough to ensure it was wedged on with no danger of coming off or without piercing the front of his skull. As the arm thrust forward and back, forward and back… The head - lifeless eyes open and unblinking - pounded up against Sarah's pussy at the perfect height for her ex's nose to occasionally penetrate her.

Not for the first time, tears streamed down her face.

Satisfied with the speed of head she was getting - a joke he had already laughed at - the clown set the remote control down on the bench, next to her face, before pulling out his semi-erect penis.

'You look thirsty,' he said.

With dick in hand, he aimed it towards her face before letting his piss flow. Just as her urine had splashed all over him, so now did his piss soak her. In an effort to get away from it, she turned her head from side to side but there was no angle she could get where it wasn't hitting her in the mouth. For every dribble she spat out, some was swallowed.

'Suck me clean,' he ordered her.

Sarah looked him dead in the eyes. Her own eyes, red-raw and watery, stinging from the dehydrated urine. The force of the head hitting her from behind, rocking her body.

'Suck me clean,' he ordered.

Sarah looked at his now-hard dick. The eye of which was crusty with dried semen from where he'd not cleaned properly the first time he'd ejaculated. The shaft still stained in patches of brown and red. She looked back to his face.

'Suck my fucking cock, bitch.'

She said again, stuttering as the head continued pounding her, 'Please let me out...'

He smiled. 'Please let me out, *sir*.'

The head continued hitting her from behind.

Contact.

Contact.

Contact.

Contact.

Its nose, on occasion, still just about penetrating her pussy.

Contact.

Contact.

Contact.

The clown spoke again, 'Well?'

She swallowed hard.

'Please let me out, *sir*,' he told her again.

Sarah closed her eyes.

Contact.

Contact.

Contact.

Contact.

She said, 'Please let me out, sir.'

'No!' The clown laughed, 'Joke's on you bitch! You aren't ever being let off this bench. You're mine now…'

Tears.

Contact.

Contact.

Contact.

Contact.

'Now suck my fucking dick! Do a real good job and I might let you out of the restraints as your reward!' he told her as he inched his cock ever closer to her mouth. Resigned to the fact it was happening whether she wanted it or not, she opened her mouth and closed her eyes. The dirty, erect penis pushed past her lips and slid down the length of her wet tongue… The tastebuds tingled at the foul taste.

Blood.

Contact.

Shit.

Contact.

Semen.

Contact.

Contact.

Contact.

She tried not to gag and she found herself wishing for it to just be over with.

She said again, 'Please let me out, sir…'

The clown laughed. For the first time since they had first met, the once-client saw something he had never seen before. Weakness. A woman broken, completely subservient to him now. He didn't smile. He kept his expression stern despite the jovial make-up of the clown painted onto his face. The restraints would stay until he grew bored and *that* he didn't see happening any time soon.

Banned Books
Too Extreme For Amazon

Unfortunately Amazon won't permit certain material on their website anymore. Because they find it offensive it means you cannot possibly enjoy it either. Personally I think that's stupid and I refuse to let anyone tell me what I can and cannot write just as you, the readers, shouldn't let people tell you what you're supposed read.

From here on in, I will be posting my extreme horror stories to my Fan-Club for members to enjoy as well as printing them into paperback format to sell on my store front. As well as new stories, my store and fan-club also contain the stories already banned on Amazon.

Just because literature is being censored, it doesn't mean we have to listen.

Want to read more stories like this and other Matt Shaw titles before they're released on Amazon?

Check out the fan club now. Stories every month!

https://www.patreon.com/TheMattShaw

Banned Books are currently available on my ETSY store:

https://www.etsy.com/uk/shop/ShawThingByMatt

With thanks to the following supporters:

Jessica Stewart, Jinx Da Clown, Briana Mishel, Jennifer Crawford, Debra Bergevin, Colleen Cassidy, Christine Feldon, Frank Meyers, Lauriette Hutzler, Daryl Duncan, Gilly Adam, Sophie Hall, Jennifer Pelfrey, Caroline Simmons-Hall, Melissa Kazas, Michael Fowler, Claire Amstrong-Brealey, Kevin Doe, Betty Lynn, Leanne Pert, Nancy Loudin, Karen McMahon, Breanna, Kelly Rickard, Christa Allin, Tammy Evens, Lance Kriegsfeld, Patty Jamison, Yvette Grimes, Mason Sabre, Hollyanne Trombley, Lollie Martin, Jennifer Risley, Anna Garcia-Centner, Martin Payne, Chrille Andersson, Angela McBride, Kim Tomsett, Andrea Stevenson, Debbie Dale, Jennifer Eversole, Andy Astle, Cece Romano, Nicola Kidd, Sanitarium Magazine, Alicia Green, Tim Feeley, Michelle Bersani, Joan MacLeod, Iain Rob Wright, Joy Boysen, Jarod Barbee, Andrea Dutton, Sue Newhouse, Christine Wickham, Travis James Armstrong, Lisa Gatzen, Ian Clayton, Alicia Jenkins, Marie Shaw, April J, Chuck Buda, Michelle Clevenger, Rebecca Thompson, Paula Limbaugh, Courtnee Fallon Rex.

https://www.patreon.com/TheMattShaw

www.mattshawpublications.co.uk

www.facebook.com/mattshawpublications

https://www.etsy.com/uk/shop/ShawThingByMatt

Printed in Great Britain
by Amazon

86518288R00077